NOTHING IS BEAUTIFUL

NOTHING IS BEAUTIFUL

By Ray Harris-Keim

Cassial Books · Lawrence, Kansas · 2021

Nothing Is Beautiful

by Ray Harris-Keim

Published by
Cassial Books
Lawrence, Kansas
www.cassialbooks.com

ISBN: 978-1-7368180-0-8 trade paperback
 978-1-7368180-1-5 electronic book

First printing

MANUFACTURED IN THE UNITED STATES OF AMERICA

Book cover by AuthorsHQ.com

Dedicated to my amazing father, who has always been there to inspire me throughout my life, and to my mother, whose support and love has driven me to accomplish my dreams.

Learn more about me at https://rayharriskeim.com

CONTENTS

1	My Town	3
2	Manhattan	16
3	Crimson Rails	29
4	Consequences	36
5	Ricky	43
6	The Train Job	49
7	The Pyres	58
8	The Lions Call	63
9	Digging Graves	69
10	Kansas City	76
11	Porter	86
12	The Coffee House	99
13	In the Night	112
14	One Last Ride	121
15	A Game of Dice	130
16	Control	139
17	In the End	147
18	Open Doors	154

NOTHING IS BEAUTIFUL

CHAPTER ONE

MY TOWN

AS I GAZED DOWN MASS STREET, WITH ITS CARCASSES of rusted abandoned cars, I listened to the loud celebration behind me. From where I stood, I could look all the way down that old weed-littered street to where the city hall stood beside the bridge and the call of the Kansas River became its roaring voice. Thick grass grew around its foundation, and the vines that tried to strangle it crawled up the building's body and stretched over it like blood vessels.

"What are you doing out here, Sharkey? Daydreamin' again?"

I tilted my chin toward Mama's voice. When she sang too loud or let her temper get the better of her, it was a noise like a split log crackling in a hearth. Still, it brought those who heard it in the night a feeling of warmth; it protected those it reached. My mother's name is Luciana Sharkey, known to her people as Mama, even though she's only mine by blood. It never bothered me that she was mother to so many; we are a family after all, every single man and woman in this town—the best of us, and the worst of us too.

"The usual. Reverend Sharp was readin' scripture again. He said somethin' like 'Uh,...this rough magic I here abjure,' and, 'when I have required some heavenly music, which even now I do, to work mine end upon'...and...oh I forget the rest. See, Mama, I came out here to wonder what it meant, cuz it don't mean shit to me."

I mocked the words of God openly and without remorse. It's in the moments that follow when I betrayed my true reason for ducking out onto the street: a joint's burning ember held up in the night between two of my fingers.

Mama only rolled her eyes and turned toward the door from which she'd come. The glow of the interior light bled through the dark, and inside I could still hear the old man preaching from the front of the bar. All that was left of that bar's first name was a single word that time had attempted to erase from the building forever: Free. Now the folks of Lawrence called it Free Place, and they'd collect there in the mornings for drink and food before the scrappers left. It was a large structure of red brick and vine, where a balcony stretched over a worn cement porch framed with benches—a decent place to watch the town's bridge and be ready for assault.

Mama's firm voice snuck up on me as my mind wandered.

"Come inside and sit at the table with your Papa. It's Oil Day, and you know how he feels about you and the scrappers sneakin' into the medical herbs. Now I won't be tellin' him...but I'd wipe that dopey smirk off your face if I were you." She waggled an orange brow, all-knowing grin playing over her face as she squeezed her wide hips back through the crack in the door.

Oil Day. Only the ancient trees in the streets had been alive long enough to have witnessed its inception: Two hundred years ago today, the last oil reserve in the world ran dry.

As I followed behind her, I was welcomed by a crowd all talking at once—some overjoyed by the celebration, others by their own semi-private conversations. Altogether, Lawrence sheltered three-hundred-odd human inhabitants—a mixture of races, genders, and cultures—but only a hundred of those were able-bodied scrappers, and even fewer could handle themselves in a fight. Most of the scrappers were in the bar that night, all of them with their ancient pistols on their hips and a beer in their hands.

I inclined my chin toward several unshaven faces as I passed by, and many of them raised their glasses in sloppy, drunken cheers to my father's name. A boy no older than three sat on the welcoming lap of an upstairs lady—one trained for making the nights just a little less lonely. She was teaching him to read, though I wondered if she knew how herself. Not many of us could say without lying that we could make sense of the written word. Only the preacher, the schoolteacher, and a few of the townspeople did. It didn't make any difference—we'd lost our town's library in a raid, and we only had about ten books left. They were all history books, or so the preacher claimed. Those few of us that could, liked to read the stories etched in the signs around town. Every few buildings had one, and there the people from before the safe cities told of their town's original founding, of the hardships those people endured, and of a man named William Quantrill.

Jack, our leader, used to boast that he could take Quantrill down with both his eyes closed in a quick draw, but none of us really knew much about that world before the uprising.

Several minutes passed before I saw my father through the crowd. Instead there was loud, tuneless singing, brief snippets of news, far too many heard jokes with lost resolve, and stories with no ends. Jack looked through me with steely blue eyes from his makeshift throne at the back of the room, his dark hair framing sunken cheeks. His three best soldiers sat beside him. I nodded at each. "Miss Porter, Ricky, Watson." Then a barely audible sigh escaped me as I came to my father's turn.

"Jack," I said too pointedly.

"It's Papa Shark, dammit, boy." He took a long swig of his drink, and my mother's voice scolded me through the noise— though I had already moved away to find my seat at the end of the long table.

"You'll call him that, please," she said.

I rolled my eyes, reaching over the table for a glass and a pitcher of beer the bartender, Davy, had delivered.

"The day he picks a less stupid name for himself will be the day I call him by it. No sooner."

"He's still your father—and the leader o' this town."

"And I show my respect by keepin' outta his place—and his politics." I raised my glass.

The beer we brewed ourselves, the old stainless-steel drum and mechanics of the brewhouse visible from behind a tall panel of glass in the back of the room. She was ancient now, and rumor has it she had been there hundreds of years before we came along—this town too. Both were remnants of the past that time had spared, perhaps to remind us that not even fire can ruin this earth forever. I think the plains are a testament to that, the trees that grew up from the ashes of the annihilated city streets, the animals that returned from near extinction to take back what was first theirs. They all flourished after the people fled. Animals that were left to die when the safe cities closed now roamed free, comfortable in the tropical climates that developed throughout the U.A. There are herds of zebras on the plains, prides of lions, and gazelle. There are even monkeys here now, animals that never lived here before. All in all, nature proved that no amount of human interference could stop it.

I looked up as Tim Sharp, the preacher, began his sermon again—even though his voice was more muddled by booze than it was before:

> And so the Lord spoke, and He said,
> "Come, let's away to prison;
> We two alone will sing like birds i' the cage:
> When thou dost ask me blessing, I'll kneel down,
> And ask of thee forgiveness: so we'll live,
> And pray, and sing, and tell old tales, and laugh
> At gilded butterflies, and hear poor rogues
> Talk of court news."

He accentuated his sermon's ending with a raised glass, nearly empty, foam clinging still to his gray beard, and a crinkle of undeniable joy in the corner of his one remaining eye. All of us cheered—some to one god, others to many, and even more of us to gods the old world had not known. Whatever the hell that crazy old man was talking about, they were the words of his god, and who were we to say they weren't true?

"All right, thank you, Preacher." My father cleared his throat as he rose to address the scrappers. "Tonight we gather here in this sacred space to honor not the riots that tore our cities down, not the walls the soldiers put up to protect themselves, not the great portals that the government built, nor the planet they promised those portals would take us to...no, tonight we celebrate the day they closed the gates of the safe cities for good, and we celebrate this day because we prevailed, we celebrate this day because our ancestors survived when they should have died. So I say to the gods now, show us into the next wasteland and we will conquer it!" He brought his palms down over the long table before him to thunderous applause.

Then, as the applause faded, he continued. "Now. We got some other things to discuss this evenin'—certain matters I'd like to bring to everyone's attention. First and foremost, our herd's come down with something, no doubt a sickness they caught from the cattle in Kansas City. The feedlots are getting bigger, and the closer they encroach upon our territory, the closer we need to watch our livestock. Next week we're shearing sheep. We're gonna need all hands available to assist, and everything packed up for market..."

I wasn't listening anymore. I had unfocused my eyes and let my mind wander. I thought about this day and what it really meant.

It began with the great oil crisis. After the panic started, the United Alliance scientists went to work searching for alternative life-bearing planets so that the human race could be preserved. The portals were huge machines that used wormhole technology to transport passengers from one location to another. They were supposed to be built in all the major cities across the world. These locations would be fortified, expanded, and deemed *safe cities*. The portals, however, were so expensive to build and maintain that the government decided only one would be allotted to each state. A new panic began the day that announcement was made, and like a match had been lit inside an anthill, the people fled in droves across the country, all of them sure in their hearts that salvation awaited them behind those towering walls.

The people were told that an earthlike planet had been discovered by United Alliance research teams and that the portals would deposit them safely onto their new world to live out the rest of their days in peace. Of course what they really meant was "anyone who had the money." The cowardly president of that era was the first to depart. The masses never heard from him or his team again. The president who was elected afterward tried his best to fix what his predecessor had done, but unfortunately not even he could bring us back from the brink of annihilation.

Violent protests between the citizens and the government broke out as the conditions inside the cities grew worse. The problem was that more people wanted through the safe city gates than they could hope to hold, and soon water and food shortages forced the government to close the gates for good. They sent road trains (huge trains constructed of tractor-trailer trucks) across the U.A. to offer anyone who wanted it a last chance at salvation in the cities that still had room. Some were sent in ships on one-way trips to our allied countries and their portals, never to be heard from again.

Only five functioning portal cities remained in the United Alliance when the smoke from the riots cleared: Kansas City; Washington, D.C.; Dallas; L.A.; and San Francisco. There are rumors of some still standing in Mexico City, Montreal, and Vancouver, but beyond that, the world outside of the U.A. is a mystery to us. Some of the cities were taken by force, others were made to abandon their portals when malfunctions could not be repaired and supplies became too scarce.

When the doors to the safe cities closed for the last time, those of us left out here, unable to reach the roads, unwilling to leave our properties—or our lives—or too ill to claim the sanctuary they desperately desired, were consequently abandoned. To prevent meltdowns, the government soldiers shut down the nuclear power plants one by one, and we were left without protection or medical aid. Some alternative power plants were left in the control of the townspeople; and Lawrence, the town where I was born and that I called my home, was blessed to have the river and a hydro plant. Generations passed like this, and although the government hoped that The Nothing would dispose of the loose ends they left, that was not our fate.

If you were lucky, you'd end up somewhere like Lawrence, where the boss kept his people safe and occupied our days with scrapping—collecting old remnants of the lost world for trade or for use in the encampment. The scrap we melted down into ingots of varying worth, to be used as currency and later returned to its prior state. Crafters could use it for just about anything—repairing buildings, ammunition, carts, food containers. If you weren't so lucky, you ended up somewhere else, somewhere the people who got too lost went to lose themselves further till they weren't even really humans anymore.

There's a lot of places like that, towns where the leaders pick at their own like vultures, where only the strongest survive and the weak end up tortured, raped, slaughtered, and cannibalized. Eudora, Lecompton, Perry, Lawrence, we turned out all right for the most part, made deals with as many devils as was necessary. We raided when we needed supplies.

Out here, a universal desire to survive finally trumped any preference or dislike in race, sexuality, gender, or religion. We are all equally fucked and doomed to fade away as dust unto The Nothing.

Suddenly the front doors clattered open, painted glass reverberating against the stucco walls, and a new kind of quiet fell over the crowd. The only sound in the bar was the hushed chatter shared between the two young men who'd just entered.

"Isaac, Nadine, where the hell have you two been? You left for that scrap site a week ago, said you'd be back no more than three days..." Jack's deep growl of a voice shook the tabletop as his gaze cut through the crowd. The boys hardly seemed to notice, both of them the picture of jubilance as they skipped up the aisle toward our table. I had never seen those brothers look so happy.

The older, Nadine, was the first to speak, his green eyes alight with news I could tell he was anxious to share with the room. Their black hair lay strewn over sweaty foreheads. "We got confirmation there's a safe city train packed with supplies comin' up our way, boss," Nadine said. "Got bullets, batteries, and everything. And they aren't waitin' for market day neither. This train's special. Our informants say it's stocked up fuller than usual and they've gone and changed up their arrival dates to confuse us." And before we knew it, we couldn't rightly tell which of the brothers was telling the tale.

"Let's get the boys together, c'mon Papa Shark. We can get a charge in place on the tracks, be there to take out the farmers that morning, and stand in for 'em when the train arrives. Those U.A. soldiers won't know what hit 'em. We got plenty o' time!"

The room buzzed with an unsettled muttering, some already reaching for their guns and checking for spare bullets. Others seemed less impressed. Jack, meanwhile, had become lost in thought, a manner of unrest I'd not yet seen in him. Mama stood abruptly, one hand waving about beside me, gesturing to summon others to their feet. She had been taking over for Papa a lot recently, and I was starting to wonder if I was the only one who noticed.

"C'mon then, you know the drill," she said.

"We've got a ditch dug under the tracks. Tatiana, Porter, Sharkey, you three are the smallest. You will man that ditch and get into whatever car stops above you. Remember, I don't want no funny business, Sharkey. There's no gettin' through those other doors without a safe city chip. I don't care what kinda crazy experiment you got cooked up in that shed, this will be a clean run. We don't get greedy. Whatever they got in that train car is enough for us. It always has been, and it always will be. Now I'm gonna need thirty more good fighters for this job. If you are interested, saddle up your horses, and get ready for some scrappin'. We'll need all the extra bullets we can get. We only got a couple days." She nodded toward the door while the assembled scrappers, men and women who'd done this job a hundred times already, stumbled to their feet. Mama spoke for Jack when he couldn't find words. Tonight, he stayed quiet as I'd ever heard him, something complicated happening behind his eyes. I said nothing as I rose to get ready.

The air outside was warm and thick with fog, all manner of night critters calling out through the dark as half a moon peered through accumulating clouds. "Looks like it will be another wet ride," I said to no one in particular, though the path toward the stables was busy with others all fetching their horses too. I approached my palomino pony, Buddy, and gathered his tack in silence. It's then, in the midst of the commotion, that I caught the tail end of a conversation in the stall beside me, the older of the two brothers from before rambling on about Manhattan, Kansas, in hushed tones.

"There's an army base in Junction City... ain't nobody there to stop us from diggin' that stuff up. They say there's all kinds of shit buried underneath: battery packs, ammo, weapons, body armor, even food."

Isaac cut in as he jerked the leather strap of his horse's girth tight. "C'mon, Nadine, you can't be serious. Papa Shark will never go for that. The old man might be losin' his touch, but he ain't stupid. Everybody knows they got silverbacks in Manhattan. Plus ain't that shit about Junction City just stories?"

"It's there," I cut in, knowing then they'd overlooked my presence in the barn altogether. "So say we don't tell the old man." They both jumped in their boots, both sets of wild eyes turning as they confessed their apologies. I waved them off. "No, no, none of that now. Let's do it. Let's raid that bunker full of guns for the train job. There's somethin' I need on that train, see, and I got myself a plan to get it, one Jack won't much appreciate. It requires an awful lotta firepower to pull off. So go on and get some people together and we'll ride out. Just don't go hollering about it, understand? Don't tell Mama, neither."

The two exchanged a simple look, but I hardly cared. I knew

what the scrappers thought of me: that I was spoiled, distracted from the cause, too obsessed with my dream of walking them all through a portal to be a proper leader. I glanced off toward the slightly skewed roof of the shed I'd built off the brewery's front and the tarnished lock that kept my secrets hidden within it.

"C'mon, Sharkey, That'd be a three-day hard ride at least one way, and with that little pony of yours slowin' us down, yer talkin' more like four. Papa Shark might be old, but he's bound to notice his own son gone for a whole week." It was the one who'd wondered if the story was even true—Isaac—who spoke then, though I could see in his eyes that adventure called to him that night.

I flashed my teeth under the shadow of my brimmed hat, oily red hair hiding whatever that look meant as I turned away again. "Just get yer damn horses ready and fetch some scrappers for the hunt. I promise it'll all be worth it when we've got that bunker open. Jack won't be mad if we bring back a good haul. You just let me worry about him."

They nodded together, turned away, and led their saddled mounts into the shadowy street in search of others, though not nearly an hour passed before a crowd began to gather outside the stables. I had just finished packing up my saddle bags when I heard the familiar bark of a voice in the doorway.

"What the fuck's all this about?" Kent and Ricky were at the head of the group, Ricky being the one who was hollering and the one I turned to face then, my shoulders as squared as I could get them. Even so, I only came up to about the middle of Ricky's chest, and he already had a palm resting over the hilt of his pistol. Ricky was older than me, stronger than me, too, his tousled brown hair cut short under his leather hat and his wild eyes fierce under angry brows.

"You sendin' these boys out to their death after some shit story?! You ain't in charge around here yet, Sharkey, and soon enough that old man o' yours won't be neither. We ain't blind, we have seen the way he lets Mama walk all over him in those

meetings. He don't do nothing anymore but sit on his ass in that
bar, so it's Mama's word we follow now. Least she ain't afraid to
talk. Now, she sent us out to get scrap, and that's it. Got it, boy?
Ain't nothin' in Junction City 'cept sick folk, and Mama won't
be so kind should you go and get her best scrappers killed by a
bunch of monkeys in Manhattan!"

I was trying hard not to flinch every time a fleck of his spit
landed on my cheek.

"What part o' don't tell no one did you two mis-hear?" I
side-eyed the boys before addressing Ricky. "Look Ricky, there's
still people loyal to Jack, me included, and I don't think they'd
be too happy to learn you're talkin' like this. What would Porter
say?" I was getting angry then as the crowd began to turn on
my father. How could they do that to him? A man who'd risked
his life on more than a dozen occasions for the whole of them. I
turned away, grabbing for my pony's reins and tossing them over
his neck. I kept my head up, though I reckon I didn't look half as
together as I thought I did.

"Whoever wants to come can come, and those will be the
people who get praised after we come back with a whole shit
load o' weapons. The rest of you…the rest of you can piss off for
all I care."

Ricky snarled, teeth clenched, pistol just begging to be
drawn as he stepped nearer. Kent, whose smaller frame moved
forward in sync with Ricky's, reached out to keep the other man
contained. "You just wait till Mama hears about this, boy. You
may think you are somethin' special, but you and that old man
o' yours will share the same fate." Ricky and Kent turned away,
no doubt to track down Mama, and before I could stop them
they'd disappeared into the massing crowd. For the first time, I
experienced doubt, and as others stepped forward to either join
or betray me, I tried my best to keep emotion off my face.

Nadine came forward first, he and his younger brother both.
"Sorry about lettin' the secret plan outta the old hat box, but we
ain't afraid o' no gorillas, Sharkey. We will ride with you." They

passed me by, one of each of their hands clasping me roughly on the shoulder in a show of alliance as they went for their mounts. Several sneering faces followed after Ricky, and each of them I attempted to categorize in my mind under threat: Mayra, a beefy woman with big arms and bigger thighs, gave me a grunt. I was blessed with a moment of hope before she turned away to follow Ricky into the night. My chest deflated, as another three I couldn't recognize in the shadows turned away from me.

Suddenly Tatiana found my eyes in the crowd, and what hope was robbed from me returned. As she approached, she leaned in close, her baby blue dress gathered up around her thighs, as she whispered, "I'll find Miss Porter, now. She'll know what to do. If there's one thing my lady's best at, it's wranglin' up a group of misbehavin' men." Her dark skin shone like gold in that light, her bright eyes brimmed with compassion that I never could understand. That woman could have soothed a snarling tiger into submission if she tried, though she wasn't a warrior by any means. She was too fragile, too much like a painting, with her curly brown hair all done up in waves over her ears. She was strong and popular though, and her rallying at my side meant others might follow.

I nodded in thanks to her silently, and was approached by another unlikely ally. "Reverend Sharp." I bowed my head in respect for the graying man before me.

Against his chest he clutched his holy book, the leather of it worn, the title page missing, and the paper it was made from yellow with age. He stared at me with his one good eye, then very carefully, and with a bent knuckle tough and calloused, tilted my chin up toward him. "My boy," he started, coughing through his words, but saying them as always, like they were from the mouth of God. "I would not wish for any companion in the world but you." As he finished, he smiled, and almost all of his teeth, though they are dark and occasionally missing, showed.

"Um…Thanks, sir, I think." The last part I only added once he'd gone off for his horse.

Finally Porter's voice came through the chatter. "I'm gonna beat you boy! What the hell were you thinkin'? Getting Ricky all wound up is one thing...." She grabbed for one of my ears and I winced away from her, rubbing at it. She had both her fists on her narrow hips, her gun belt over her red pants, and a thick leather jacket tight around her flat chest and her muscled arms. I could tell she was coming along before she said so. I could see it in her fiery eyes and the way she had her blond hair all tied up in a bun under her hat.

"I'm sorry." I ducked as she went for my ear again. "Lay off my ear, woman!"

She cursed under her breath and nodded toward the stalls behind me. "You know I ain't one for getting yer old man angry, but the preacher's on this fool's errand o' yours now, and ya know I couldn't let my father go off without me. Who's gonna translate his sermons right?" She grinned, flashing her teeth in a way that brought her beauty out. It was a tough beauty, hardened by a rough world and softened only by the gentle love of her wife. Tatiana fell in step behind her, and I barely had time to call back a quiet "Don't think the translatin' will do much good, but glad to have ya" before she had gone into the barn.

They all found their way to me that night, and altogether seven of us rode out onto those endless, mist-covered prairies. As we rode, Tatiana doubled up on Porter's saddle with her arms around her lover's waist, the always cocky and troublemaking Wes and the brothers behind me.

The preacher called out into the dark that swallowed us.

> But thy eternal summer shall not fade
> Nor lose possession of that fair thou ow'st;
> Nor shall Death brag thou wander'st in his shade,
> When in eternal lines to time thou grow'st:
>> So long as men can breathe, or eyes can see,
>> So long lives this, and this gives life to thee.

CHAPTER TWO

MANHATTAN

THUNDER CALLED OUT OVER THE ROLLING KANSAS hills, taunting us with threats of rain and howling winds. The air was heavy and warm, and the horses beneath us tossed their heads in discomfort. The sun was just trying to make it through the storm clouds, and it was enough to make the damp grass look like fire on the horizon.

"The 18? Why ain't we takin the highway?" Porter was yelling, reins caught up in one fist while the other gestured in a different direction. Already we could see the road through a line of trees.

I shook my head, pulling my pony around to halt the group before we got too close. "No fuckin' way are we paying to get through that toll. You know the 70's controlled by the U.A., they got soldiers all up an' down there. We ain't riskin' that. Hell, half o' ya have bounties on your heads. We take 18 all the way to Junction City. We skirt Topeka, get through Manhattan, and it's smooth ridin' from there."

"Well, that's a shit plan, but I guess it'll do."

Porter was shaking her head now, the mess of hair on top threatening to tumble back over her shoulders as she kicked her horse up into a gallop and went ahead, all the time yelling objections in my direction. She was the only person I reckoned who had the guts to talk to Jack's son that way. Still, there wasn't anything I could do, no alternative route that would keep my people any safer. In truth, there was only so much you could do now to keep from getting killed by one thing or another. The rest of the group seemed less perturbed, and Tatiana even smiled reassuringly at me as she passed, arms still wound around her lover's waist.

Isaac watched me from my left, his sorrel mare chewing at her bit as her rider's green eyes followed mine. He was young, young enough to still look kind, in The Nothing. He had never been broken, he had never known loss, nor had the life he'd been given taken from him that light inside. I tried my best to return the wide smile that he offered me, but mine came off more awkward than anything.

His voice was chipper, bouncing with the gait of his mare. "Ya know whenever I get scared, I think about them old video documentaries we found. There's one we play every now and then on the big screen in the little theater. I don't know what the story's really called, but the hero, Clint Eastwood, I think about him. What would he do? And I ain't so scared anymore."

Thunder encroached, building to a peak as lightning illuminated the gravel road between us, and our mounts tensed. "I ain't scared," I said, glancing away from him and toward the tall prairie grass and the pale rock beneath the earth that split the hills in half. Now that road was just a ghost. Nearly gone, buried under dirt and gravel, and swallowed by the land.

"It's just a mission like any other." Isaac smiled, head bowed in a nod as he moved on toward his brother, who rode with Porter at the lead.

I couldn't help but let my thoughts wander that day, as all around us The Nothing went on with its business, not caring who we were or where we were going. Maybe Isaac was right. Maybe I was scared, not of the gorillas, not even of the feral people in Topeka, but of the return, of what might meet me at the gates of Lawrence. Beside us, through the tall brush and the taller trees, the Kansas River ran high, lapping at the banks as rain engorged it.

The journey itself was long and damp. Topeka was of course the first thing we had to worry about, and as we approached its edge, even the horses seemed to tense their muscles. Instincts drove goosebumps over our flesh, and the air felt colder the closer that we came. When we could finally see the chain link and the barbed wire that fortified the perimeter, other sights could not be avoided: rotting corpses of trespassers had been strung through the gates by their intestines; gates had been left open, a dare for anyone to attempt to cross through that wasteland on to the gray scape of trash and filth that welcomed them. As we rode closer to the city, we could see feral figures scrambling into the shadows to wait for us. The trail we followed turned away from that place finally, and I was able to breathe again.

As we left, screams echoed out through the desolate streets, proof that some excuse for life still dwelled within somewhere. None of us stopped. And even though eyes glanced toward me, yearning for the cue to leap into action, all of them already knew my answer. There was no hope for those souls the cannibals caught. Even if we'd tried, we would have joined them in the end, outnumbered and unable to kill enough to make a difference. Eventually the screaming stopped. It always did.

■

On the third night, we came across a fortified orchard. U.A. snipers peered at us from blinds, and farmers watched us suspiciously as we crossed by the tall fence at its edge. The trees they tended held huge apples, and I could almost hear the stomachs of my crew start growling. Perhaps the snipers heard too. Maybe that's why fingers adjusted their grips on their rifles and stern voices called out warnings in the dark.

"Move along!"

We kept our heads down. Some faces even turned away so as not to call attention to themselves. Then as quickly as it had appeared, the orchard, with its tall, bright lights and its towers, was far behind us.

Wes approached me on my left some time after, his shaggy mop of brown hair clinging to his angled cheeks in the rain. He seemed tense. I made note of it and glanced at him with a concerned expression in the moonlight.

"We gotta stop for the night boss. I saw lion tracks back there, fresh ones from the looks of it. I say we set up camp on that cliff up yonder, start a fire to spook the pride."

I pulled back on my reins, voice as strong as I could make it as I searched the shadows for the others.

"All right, people, we got lions on our trail. See that cliff up there? That will be camp. *Porter.*" I raised my voice, gesturing to my side.

As she was summoned, Tatiana was half asleep against her strong shoulders. Porter looked up at me with worry in her eyes.

"Start makin' a fire, a big one, and leave the horses tied with slip knots so they can run if the pride finds us. Runnin' horse—"

Porter finished my sentence, confirming she'd been an excellent choice for my second in command.

"—is a good way to distract a lion. I gotcha kid. What'r you gonna do?"

I swallowed hard, hand down on my pistol to check it before replying.

"I'm gonna check the perimeter...ya know...leader stuff." I winked, though the lopsided smirk that accompanied the look didn't seem to sell my newfound confidence. Porter watched me with hard eyes but turned away without arguing, galloping up toward the peak I'd referenced. Wes followed her reluctantly, and after trying his hardest to stay at my side, Isaac too, then his brother, and then the preacher. The old man called back something or other about thanks and thanks, and then I was very much alone at the base of the mound of dark rock. For a moment I couldn't think to move, though my pony took it upon himself to force me.

Suddenly I was moving very fast toward the dim lantern lights that hung from the others' saddles, and a choice curse word later I had managed to halt my pony's attempts to join its companions.

"Cut that shit out, Buddy," I grumbled as I swung down and tugged the animal into a slow walk. I had my flashlight out now, and although it was always best to reserve it for emergencies, I was on a hunt for tracks. A lesser primate howled somewhere nearby. My eyes jerked toward the racket it had caused and the rustle in the trees to the left of the campsite. The cliff rose up to my right, then the path curved around its front and headed down into the forest.

I found what I was looking for at the edge of the trees, there between two tall ferns. Fresh tracks twice the size of my hands. No claws. Lions.

By the time I had turned and made it back as quietly as possible around the cliff to the flat ledge where the others had settled down, they were sitting around a fire, and it hissed at me. Maybe that would have been less startling, had it not been coupled with the click of Porter's pistol cocking not two inches from my face. Apparently I had been quieter than I thought.

"Easy, Porter...damn..."

"Well." She said, holstering her gun and pulling her shoulders into a tight shrug, "if you'd been a lion, I woulda shot ya dead."

I mirrored her grin and the night mulled on. Tatiana fell asleep first, burdened no doubt by thoughts of the town she'd left behind and the trouble she'd be in when she returned to it, then the preacher, Porter, and the boys. Finally only Wes and I remained conscious.

"C'mere," he whispered suddenly, and I could feel my brows knitting together.

"What is it?"

"Just look," he said, nostrils flaring. A hand reached up to brush his brown bangs out of his face, and he gestured down the cliffside. I moved across toward him, half on my belly, so I could peer over the edge. A herd of unsuspecting white-tailed deer had gathered in the prairie beneath us, and if you watched carefully, you could see several lionesses slowly approaching through the tall grass. The deer, unfortunately, did not have the advantage that Wes and I shared. Finally, as the hunt's end grew near, I rolled away.

"Better them than us," I whispered, turning my attention

toward my saddlebags as I dug out a pot and a can of something
to eat.

Wes watched me, a look of sallow understanding stretched
over his high cheeks like a mask.

I use the can as a not-so-sentimental apology, waving it
around a bit. "You want some soup?" It was all I could do to tell
him I felt some manner of unrest at seeing those deer mauled to
death, but out here, there wasn't much leeway for a person to get
all sappy over shit like that. He seemed to understand, and for a
while, we sat in silence, watching the bubbles in the pot of soup
pop. Wes had returned to his vantage point, partly leaning over
the bluff's edge so he could keep an eye on the animals below.

"The Nothin' will just swallow you up if you ain't careful,
won't it, Sharkey?" he asked abruptly, causing my spoon to pause
in its journey to my mouth.

I sighed.

"Somethin' like that. Now get away from the edge. Breeze
picks up and it'll be you those girls will be eatin', not deer."

We didn't see the pride again on that trip.

Four days riding and we only really slept that one time. We
galloped mostly. In fact I felt I couldn't gallop another second
when the silhouette of Manhattan peeled away through the
clouds, framing itself against the light from the receding moon.
In the early dawn, the jagged edges of dead buildings looked
haunted. They watched us. Something watched us.

"We made it!" Wes rejoiced, and I scowled hard under the rim
of my hat.

"Shut yer mouth. We ain't made it yet. We got two miles at
least. A lot could happen in two miles." A dread was settling
over my heart. It was the kind of panic that made it difficult to
breathe, and every sound along the abandoned highway those
last two miles made my heart leap in my chest. The rain fell off
and on. The horses trotted through it, unaffected, and as the
sun began to rise and warm the road, a fog gathered under our
animals' feet.

Still, the city loomed ever nearer, littered with all manner of half-eaten bodies of metal cars, buses, and bits of a world almost alien to us.

Those days it always rained. It rained when people were happy. It rained when people were sad. It rained for births and deaths and celebrations.

Without warning, from the dilapidated skeletons of two buses that fenced off the sides of the road, shapes leaped at us, dark camo cloaks thrown off onto the black tar and discarded without grace into the cracks. Horses reared, guns were drawn, voices bombarded us from all sides as a dozen men closed in.

After the initial startle had passed and one man stepped forward to introduce himself as our worst nightmare, our nemesis, our inescapable fate, a calm settled over me. It was always one of those. They always had dark eyes that had vengeance inside them, darker hair where grease clung, and a collection of loyal boys who knew no better but would inevitably turn on their heels once their leader had fallen.

So he began: "Now let me tell you all how this is gonna go down. See these parts, these parts belong to me and my boys here. Well they haven't gotten a chance to kill in quite a while, haven't gotten no women neither…" There was the sneer, the one they always wore when they thought their monologue was working us all into a state of fear. I let him go on, my people on their horses, all of them watching me, while I watched him, waiting. Maybe minutes passed by as he paced this way and that, one hand propping his coat open so I could see his weapon in its holster. Forgotten, like I wasn't good enough to deserve its being drawn. But he wasn't watching me. He was too busy thinking about what verse came next, his practiced words lacking any sort of imagination. Then my patience finally ran out. See, if there's one thing I had learned in my years growing up in The Nothing, it was this: Always kill the bad guy, and never, ever let him finish his monologue before you do.

The gunshot startled the horses, hooves clattering over bits of debris as reins were gathered and shocked eyes tried to sort out what had happened. The pistol I held in my palm felt warm and safe. I watched that man, with his black hair, his black eyes, and his cocky leer, fall backwards and topple without grace unto the road beneath him. Then, like I had known it would happen, his loyal men scattered like so many scared cockroaches into the tall prairie grass around us.

I rode on, heels nudging my horse's side as I holstered my pistol, and Porter behind me, no doubt shaking her head, muttered into the dawn, "Well, I reckon that's one way to handle it."

I couldn't help but hear something like pride in her voice.

By now I hoped that was the only way my people thought a thing like that could be dealt with. Once upon a time I'm sure folks could talk their way through anything, treaties, and empty promises of peace for their followers to holler at. But now, out here in The Nothing, either they died or you did. All the stories I read back in Lawrence, and the shows we'd scavenged to watch in our little theater all told the same stories: bad guys, good guys, everybody fights, final battle, good guy wins. The bad guy always has this moment where he talks too much, and the good guy always falls for it. He gives him a second chance and the bad guy takes his offer of forgiveness and stabs him in the back with it. I hate those fucking stories.

Before we knew it, all of us stood at the gates of Manhattan with our hearts in our throats and our hats in our hands. Something about that place made you want to mourn, even if you hadn't lost anyone yet. The skyscrapers, empty and half-broken, looked like tombstones, and the cars that lay in the streets among the worn-away storefronts with their mannequins appeared almost surreal in the morning light.

Wes spoke up again, his cocky expression gone and a look of suspicion took its place. "Ain't this the part when you say some inspiring speech that makes us all fuzzy inside?" He gave me an expecting look, gray eyes peering up through his bangs as he dropped down out of his saddle and took his place beside me.

"You really need inspirin' to shoot a bunch o' gorillas?"

He chewed on his lip, one hand tousling through his hair as he turned away muttering, "Right. No, you're right. Dunno what I was thinkin'."

Porter found me next, wearing the contemplative expression she always did, hiding behind something new…doubt maybe. "Well, how ya gonna get us through this?"

I waited too. Waited for some miraculous plan to come to me. And yet the only thing I could think to do was go forth, fearlessly. That's what my father would have done. *C'mon Sharkey…say somethin' that will let them know you ain't a coward.*

My voice became the roar of the rain as it picked up, the crash of thunder and the rattle of the wind against the metal street signs.

"Everybody dismount. We are gonna walk the horses. Try and keep 'em quiet."

Porter walked beside me, uncertainty in her eyes. The preacher watched his daughter's back as he muttered verses under his breath, though I couldn't tell if they were meant to inspire us or warn us away.

> Be not afeard. The isle is full of noises,
> Sounds, and sweet airs that give delight and hurt not.
> Sometimes a thousand twangling instruments
> Will hum about mine ears, and sometime voices,
> That, if I then had waked after long sleep,
> Will make me sleep again. And then, in dreaming,
> The clouds methought would open, and show riches
> Ready to drop upon me, that when I waked,
> I cried to dream again.

Tatiana clung to her wife's side, her features gentle, in

stark contrast to the gray, harsh world around her. Wes was
humming something under his breath; and the brothers, one of
them angrier than the other, appeared to be in the middle of a
heated dispute.

For a moment, the rain seemed to quiet, the streets seemed
still, and the air felt fresh and clean in my chest. Isaac had leaped
out in front of the group, a devilish grin on his face and both his
fists around his twin pistols. He was trying his hardest to twirl
them around and stick them back in their holsters just like his
hero. Joy overcame him when he was successful, and his brother,
eyes blissful, watched him, whatever contempt they had held
prior, gone in an instant.

"Don't worry, guys, I'll protect you! Clint Eastwood wouldn't
be afraid of no monkeys." Isaac called back to us, grinning wide,
the argument they had been in the middle of forgotten, though
Nadine did his best to pretend like he was still peeved.

"Get back here, you fuckin' idiot!"

I turned my back to the boy for a moment, walking backward
so I could give Porter a look. I shrugged my shoulders, laughter
in both our eyes.

Then there was no sound. No shape until it was upon him.
No break in what should have been eternal, peaceful still until
Nadine cried out. When I looked again, a pair of huge hands
made of black leather had consumed Isaac's tiny form, gripped
it, tore it, and sought to separate it into halves. The smile was
still there on his face when the gorilla's monstrous jaws dug in
around his throat, ripped open his shoulder, and flung him as if
he were made of straw into a brick wall behind it.

Nadine, overcome by rage and pain, pulled his gun, shouted
out in chaotic agony, and missed every one of his five shots. Any
chance at avenging his brother's death was lost. There was so
much blood. Blood in my ears, pounding, blood in the streets,
blood on the orange metal, blood on Nadine's boots. The horses
were screaming.

There was no time to retrieve his body. For there, in the space where that silverback, all ten feet of it stood, others came. These were not the creatures from the old world who were content to lie in zoos, three hundred pounds of wasted potential—no, these were truly monsters, evolved to be stronger, bigger, faster. Even their language, spoken, rough words that took on the shape of discontent, seemed too human. The gorilla who killed Isaac was seven hundred pounds at least, with arms the size of tree trunks, and eyes, those empty dark eyes. There was a Bio and Agro-Defense facility in Manhattan. That's where they had been created. Only the gods of the old world knew why. Entertainment? War? Because we could?

Three more arrived, screaming words we couldn't understand into the rain as their bodies crashed down into the street from the buildings above us. Two females flanked him now, looking down with clear disgust at the felled man who had dared step foot inside their beautiful kingdom. One bared her enormous teeth, a great howl bursting from her as balled fists hammered over her ebony breasts. We rode as fast as we could, beating our palms over the rumps of our horses as their hoofbeats echoed through the city.

This sick, twisted world had forgotten that there was a time when it was ruled by us. The people had thought that their future was made of silver buildings and computer screens, with towers that reached into the sky, cars that flew, and gray horizons instead of green ones. How wrong they'd been. Now we were like a parasite on this earth, digging through the trash of the old civilization, desperately trying to find ourselves amongst the rubble.

Even once the screams had turned to sobs and a headcount revealed Isaac had been our only casualty, it haunted us. You never know until something terrible has happened what it will feel like and how you will react. My stomach turned, my heart pounded as adrenaline surged through my body, and there, in the mud beside, me Nadine wailed into the sky. I could hear

the gorillas chanting for their victory behind us, pounding their
chests, yelling out in their wild tongue, telling us they'd won.

"Nadine," I gasped, voice broken and small. He was turned
away from me, still clutching at the earth beneath him, unable
to stand through the panic and the weight of the world that had
come crashing down over his heart.

I stood finally, my people mirroring my bowed head, my
closed eyes. Porter held her trembling wife in her arms, her
fingers lacing through the tight, black curls that framed Tatiana's
tear-stained cheeks. Wes watched me. Nadine muttered things
beneath his sobs that broke my heart. His caramel-colored skin
was still speckled by wet droplets of his brother's blood. The
preacher found me in the gathering crowd. He reached for me,
his old hand shaking as it closed over my shoulder. I could feel
the intent behind it, and even though his book of God's words
could not fix what had been broken, could not bring back what
had been taken away, he tried.

The preacher clasped his hands before himself, shoulders
braced, head held high as he spoke. His voice was bracing, stiff,
like cold air, and his silver eye looked tired, its edges wrinkled
by age.

> Cowards die many times before their deaths
> The valiant never taste of death but once.
> Of all the wonders that I yet have heard,
> It seems to me most strange that men should fear;
> Seeing that death, a necessary end,
> Will come when it will come.

"We gotta keep movin'," I called once he'd finished, clearing
my throat. The others gathered themselves up slowly, and
together, one less head than before, we moved on.

The ride went by fast, even though we rode that whole day.
Then, as if the gods had done it all on purpose, we soon stood

over a deep, unguarded pit and a wide open, forgotten bunker full of piss-all. There were no guns, there were no batteries. No, within those cold steel walls, and stacked up on shelves, and piled in the receding space where shadow lay, there was nothing but dust and rat shit, and when all I saw was my own reflection in the steel gun cabinet doors, I felt sick.

Nobody said anything. I didn't dare look my people in the eyes. We turned away, cold, wet, emptyhanded, doomed to brave the city of Manhattan yet again, with nothing but our pistols and broken spirits to protect us.

CHAPTER THREE

CRIMSON RAILS

T DIDN'T MATTER THAT WE MADE IT BACK THROUGH that city and never saw a damn sewer rat, much less a gorilla. It didn't matter because the city was taunting us. It had taken something from us and given us nothing in return, and even for that, I could not make it pay.

"Leave the fuckin' horse. We ain't got time to fight with her."

I couldn't see straight. I couldn't hear anything but Isaac's mare throwing her fit. Her ears were pinned and she was bucking, pulling as hard as she could against the ropes we'd tossed over her neck. I turned away, reins in my hands, pretending it was the cold rain that was making them shake. The others relented, allowing the rogue animal to succumb to the fear that drove her off toward the city where she'd seen her rider go last. She'd die messy, and with her went the last light in Nadine's once-bright eyes.

"'I am sorry," I said, watching the rain stream off the bill of my hat. "Y'know we couldn't wait for her to settle. We gotta get back before the train job."

It was Nadine's hands that shook now, and I knew for a fact it had nothing to do with the rain. "He had that mare since she was a two-week-old filly. Her mama died foaling, and Isaac bought her from a butcher who couldn't keep her alive. He was gonna put her to the block, keep his own kids goin', but Isaac wouldn't have it. He couldn't watch that little filly die. Took every last bit of scrap that he had to get her, and I was against it of course...." He trailed off as the others watched, all of us on edge, waiting, like he was going to crumble at any moment.

"But he got his way...." The boy's green eyes spilled over through his thick lashes and scattered tears over his dark skin like birdshot.

All we could do was keep going. The rough gusts and hard downpour were all we could hear over our horses' hooves pounding the muddy path. I had lost myself, and I wasn't sure if I would ever be whole again. Of course I had lost people before. This life out here, The Nothing takes all and gives nothing back. But it had never been like this. It had never been my fault.

We approached a forest path, and the leaves of the oaks danced under the raindrops, pale where their undersides had been thrown up in the wind. Briefly, at the head of the trail, I pulled back on my reins, halting the group and gesturing toward the shadowy foreground.

"Storm's gettin' worse. It will be an easier ride through the forest." Nobody questioned me, but that was the first time that I saw a lack of trust in their eyes. Even Porter, tugging her holsters back into place from the ride, looked up at me from under her hat with a resentment that sent chills through my body. Tatiana countered it of course, that wide smile of hers stretching over her face in hopes it would be enough to quell the fear that was blooming inside my chest. It wasn't.

I turned away from her abruptly, all of my attention on the forest whose arms stretched out around us, broken and bent into dangerous points. The horses seemed more bothered than ever once we entered, and my own pony tugged restlessly at his reins, shoulders stiff as we wound our way under fallen trees and through thick bramble patches.

"You sure this was a good idea?" Porter called over the wind that had grown only louder, now howling through the swaying branches like wolves.

I winced, turning away from a branch that the gales had tossed toward my face. I dabbed gingerly at the cut that it had made before I answered.

"Fuck if I know, Porter. I thought it'd be calmer with the trees. You reckon we should head back for the road?"

Just then, my pony halted suddenly, and I, unprepared, went rolling forward and onto my back at his stomping feet.

"*Goddammit!*" I yelled, cursing loudly. Wes hopped down to grab my arms.

"Ya all right boss?" he said, trying his best to hide his shit-eating grin. I rolled my eyes, grabbing at my pony's reins as I pushed off Wes's shoulder and into a disgruntled squat. I was half tempted to pull my skewed hat off and swat that damn pony over the nose with it.

"The hell spooked him, anyways?" Wes stood beside me now, patting comfortingly over Buddy's withers as he scanned the forest ahead. Nothing looked out of place: no cat eyes caught the light, no bit of tarp or trash had been left over from a camp, nothing bright shone, and only the shifting shadows that the storm drew over the forest floor moved.

"Who knows. I think it's the weather. Damn horse...." I waved the others on, each of their faces briefly adorned with an expression of concern. Even Nadine reached out to comb fingers through my pony's mane for a moment. I couldn't imagine what he must have thought of me, and I wondered if he'd ever look at me the way that he used to again. With admiration...or even with respect.

"Uh, Sharkey. You better get up here."

I sighed deliberately as Porter's voice called through from the trail ahead.

"No, don't tell me that shit. What 'something I need to see'? What the hell is it? I hate that."

"Well I'd tell ya if I knew what the fuck it was, jackass."

Porter caught me in the jaw with her elbow as I walked up, pony shoving his head into my back as if to accentuate their coupled annoyance with me. I knew she did it on purpose, but Porter was one of the only people I'd let bully me without retaliation. Funny how her beating me up gave me hope.

What lay crumpled in the brush before us took the breath from my lungs. It had partly been consumed by the color of the forest, but its shape remained—humanlike, its silver skin worn by weather. A hand stretched out from the vines that held its body still, and through the overcast light, I could still make out the Safe City seal that had been stamped over its breastplate.

"Holy shit. That's—that's a safe city robot. Wh-what the fuck is it doing in the middle of the forest?" I couldn't believe what I was seeing, and although it appeared the power cell had died long ago, I couldn't begin to plot all the uses it could have. My heart pounded in my chest, and an excitement I hadn't felt for a very long time found my wide, brown eyes.

"Get it outta there," I panted, leaping forward and reaching for my knife. The others followed suit, and Porter slid her pistol from its sheath.

When I glanced at her curiously, she shrugged and nodded toward the robot's lifeless form.

I turned back, knife working through the vines with haste. "It ain't gonna hurt you." But my words were lost in the chorus that had begun.

"Is it dead?"

"Why is it out here?"

"Where'd it come from?"

I replied distractedly as I tilted its blank, silver face toward me. My fingers searched over the back of its head for any access to its internal wiring. "Maybe it wandered off from 70. They got labor bots down there, don't they? Haulin' shit for 'em?"

Tatiana stepped back slowly, ensuring her wife stood between herself and the creature I knelt over. "Can it...you know...?"

"Don't be silly. Everyone knows robots can't hurt people," I said.

Wes grinned, flipping his knife over in his hand and tapping on the android's metallic head with its handle. "So what do you think? Burnt out power core? I thought these things were solar."

I nodded.

"It must've wandered into the forest, then lost battery. The trees are too thick to charge it up again, so here it is. I wonder how long it's been here." But my words lacked luster as my mind wandered freely, far away from that forest and the piece of machinery before me. After all, that robot had in its right hand a tiny chip, a little square of composite that would change everything.

"Wes...," I started, still distracted and interrupting the conversation around me without care. "Get it onto your horse. C'mon. We are taking it back to Lawrence."

Porter intervened, a snarl in her voice. She braced my shoulder to hold me back.

"Hold on there. We can't take this thing back to Lawrence. Are you crazy, kid?"

"Crazy?" I nodded for Wes to continue.

"Yeah, I said it, Sharkey. You got that kid killed back there whether you admit it or not, and now you are haulin' safe city property back to Lawrence? You know them things have tracker chips in them. Hell, soldiers are prolly on their way to pick it up right now." She looked around, as if she expected some to step out of the forest on cue.

I was still attempting to recover from the pain her first set of words had inflicted when she prompted me to reply with an expecting snort.

"C'mon, Porter, if the soldiers were gonna find it, they woulda by now. Thing's been out here for months. Tracker prolly burnt out after the solar battery lost charge and used up the backup. It's out cold till we charge it up."

"And what?" Porter queried, eyes perplexed and disbelieving. "You just happen to know how to fix it?"

"Yeah, actually I do. What did you think I do in that shed all the damn time, collages? It has a solar panel on top and four separate extension cords runnin' under the door for fuck's sake. I've been buildin somethin'." I shifted uneasily before turning away from her, further explanation abandoned.

The group exchanged questioning looks, but no one else spoke up as Wes grabbed the robot and strapped it into place on his mare's back. The horse shifted uncomfortably beneath the additional weight, but once Wes mounted, he pulled her around

into position beside me. "Your move, boss." His messy hair
fell over his eyes as he kicked his mare into a trot and moved
ahead. I remember watching the robot's face, blank silver metal
littered with raindrops, and my mind wandered again. So many
possibilities lay with that android's existence. I could only think
that perhaps Isaac hadn't died for nothing after all.

I doubted Nadine saw it that way.

Porter rode beside me. Tatiana rode with the preacher ahead
of us. Porter's eyes looked burdened, like she was fussing over
something in the back of her mind. When she caught me looking,
she straightened up in her seat, reins gathered up close.

"How ya holding up, kid?" She tucked a strand of blonde hair
back behind her ear.

I glanced up, puzzled. "Hell, Porter, ya ain't worried about
me, are ya?"

She gritted her teeth.

"Don't be a little shit. Course I worry. Hell, yer like a brother
to me. If anything ever happened..."

I cut her off, arm stretched out between our horses to rest
briefly over her shoulder. "Don't." My head ducked, ginger
bangs drawing over my eyes. Tatiana watched nervously over a
shoulder as she rode behind the preacher. I tried my best to give
her a reassuring smile before glancing back toward Porter.

"I think I'm okay, Porter...it's just...Nadine. He ain't got
nobody left and that's on me. Hell, I couldn't even save his
brother's damn horse." Porter's voice came in next, consoling, if
it could. Hell, at least she tried.

"Sharkey, listen to me. Out here in The Nothin', folk die.
Good folk, bad folk. You start blaming yourself for that now
and you won't ever stop and you won't ever lead us. That guilt
will drive you crazy. Trust me on that. I have seen it happen to
stronger men, seen it done to yer old man years ago. I was just a
kid, and he was just a man without a piece of scrap to his name.
He didn't have nobody but Mama to follow him, and my dad
and me. But one night, few months after he'd gotten together

his first group of folks, he decided we'd go on a raid. Heard of a train comin' through on a run. He'd never tried to take a train before, but he had it all worked out. Ride in at dawn with pistols drawn and surprise 'em once the soldiers got off to load supplies at the stop. I didn't get to go, but I know it went bad. Everybody died 'cept yer daddy and mine. Course the preacher came back with one less eye, and old Papa Shark, well his heart broke for the first time that day, and he came back with nothing but his people's blood on his hands. You think he didn't blame himself? Cuz he did. It nearly destroyed him. In fact he said he'd never do it again, and he closed the Free Place that night."

"What? What made him change his mind?"

"You. You were born that next day, Sharkey. And he took you out into the street, and he held you up beneath the stars, and he made a promise that he'd never let you down. You gave him the strength that he needed to try again. And that's how his crew came to be. I was little, but even I could see how proud he was of you. Whatever happens when we get back, just know that he loves you, always."

My eyes stung with tears and my chest felt tight, a feeling overtaking me that I was not too familiar with. I had never bothered to see my father in such a light as that. Suddenly Porter's snickers came through, her lips curled into a smirk beside me.

"What? Ain't ya ever seen a man cry before?"

She laughed again, grin nearly all the way across her face as she clicked her horse into a gallop to join Tatiana and her father.

"I just like seein' ya all weepy. Makes me warm inside." Her voice was distant now, but the feeling of comfort that it left behind didn't fade.

CHAPTER FOUR

CONSEQUENCES

THOUGHT A LOT ABOUT THAT STORY SHE'D TOLD ME AS we rode the last few days back to Lawrence, and I tried to hold onto the feeling of warmth that had overcome me thinking of my father holding me up to the stars like that. It wasn't enough to keep my heart from racing as we passed by the abandoned neighborhoods off Sixth Street. The concave skeletons of buildings doubled over on themselves, watched us like prowling monsters from the roadside. It wouldn't be long now. I could see the Mass Street barricade and the glint of the snipers' scopes from my saddle.

"Y'all let me do the talkin', all right? He ain't gonna be happy, but I reckon it will go over better if the story comes from me." Somehow I didn't sound as ready as I thought I was. Instead I came off scared as I felt, a tremble in my voice that I attempted to clear with a cough.

My comrades only nodded, heads bowed as we came up on the fortified wall we'd erected by the bridge. Several familiar faces greeted me as we approached.

"Welcome back, Sharkey," they sang together—snidely.

"Yer dad's pissed as a wet hornet."

Both men snickered as they hauled back the gates to let us pass.

"Yeah. Tell me sumthin' new," I said under my breath, grimacing as I led my pony around toward the stables. The others followed, each dismounting off sore asses and groaning as they started pulling saddles off. It was Porter's cursing that caught my attention though.

"What's wrong, Porter?" I was desperate for any excuse to stay in the barn and help.

Porter side-eyed me, hands busy wiping blood off her saddle

36

seat. "I lost track of the month." Was it a good enough excuse to give for not heading inside the Free Place to talk to my father? I doubted it, but tested it anyway.

"Want me to go get you something from the shop? Napkins? Pain meds? Chocolate? I can go to a totally different town somewhere really far away maybe, see if they have better supplies."

"Fuck off."

The moment we shared was brief but gentle, enough of an escape from reality to allow my breath to catch in my chest. She sighed, rubbing a palm over her stomach as she stepped up to face me.

"Go talk to your father, Sharkey." Her smile faded from her sharp jaw as she rested her hand on my shoulder.

It was a moment that would define my future. Whether I went into the Free Place that night, or, instead, avoided my father's reprimand, turned, fled from the city, and never looked back.

"But how 'bout I don't? I got an idea." Suddenly I was grinning again, the jest in my suggestion obvious and severely temporary. "What about we just saddle back up and get the fuck out of here? You and me."

She didn't have to say anything. Even before I saw her face, I knew she was giving me that look. She didn't have to shove me through the barn doors or jerk me away from the robot that Wes was hauling off his horse. She just watched me, and it was the feeling of her eyes against my back that kept me walking.

The doors of the Free Place made a horrible racket as I pushed through them, then again as my crew filed in behind me, Wes cradling the lifeless robot in his arms, Porter with her hands tucked under her armpits, Tatiana hiding behind her wife's shoulders. I watched as every single head, most hovering over beers and adorned with gaping mouths in mid conversation, turned toward us. I heard every conversation cease, and a quiet overtook the room that seemed almost supernatural. Then there was Jack, sitting in the middle of his long table with Ricky and Kent, and Mama beside him. She was the only one who looked happy to see me, and without a second thought, she rose from the table and came rushing at me, arms wide and welcoming.

She had told me once that even if a child does an unthinkably evil act, it is a mother's job to love them still, no matter what, and to the very end of all things. I hoped that she had meant that now, as I squeezed her broad shoulders, inhaled the unforgettable scent of her ginger hair, and glanced briefly into her face. I remember taking my time watching the freckles above her lids, and avoided altogether her eyes beneath them that made me feel afraid again.

Although she embraced me willingly, the act gentle and loving, trepidation still overcame me, and when my father finally rose, a cruel chill bore its way down my spine.

"Where the fuck have ya been?" The room seemed to wince as one, their expressions each reflecting the agitation of animals who had just heard thunder in the air.

"Scrappin', just like you said. Got a little distracted is all..." I hesitated, fully aware now that my father had crossed the room to stand in front of me. It was rare that he left his long table for anything, proof enough that I was in for a special sort of treat tonight.

"You been gone fer days, boy. Ya took good people, important people. We thought you was dead."

Porter was close now, and her warm breath was on my back, her sharp chin turned down, several of her blond hairs trailing toward the attractive static of my coat.

"Weren't fer nuthin', Papa," she said, voice deliberate, muscles in her jaw clenched over her last word. I could tell she was trying to sound sure, but I could also tell she wasn't. Still, it meant something that she was willing to say anything to him at all.

I intervened, picking up where Porter left off, nerves bristling at the fact that he hadn't said anything back to her yet.

"We found somethin', somethin' that could change everythin'.

I'm tellin' you for real this time. Wes, bring it here." Wes complied immediately, ducking forward to position the robot where it could be on the best display.

A universal murmur made its way around the room, followed in suit by all manner of groans, mutters, quips, and variations of the three by the crowded hall. One man cursed louder than the others, and as pistols were drawn it was obvious that fear had woken in them.

"No, no, it's okay. It ain't turned on. Not yet. You don't gotta be afraid."

"I ain't afraid." Papa Shark's voice rose above the discord, firm, unwavering, cold as ice. I felt like I was supposed to say something deep, something meaningful, but instead there was only an emptiness in my mouth, a numbness in my limbs that I think was dread.

Sometimes in life you realize a moment is happening before it's happened. You see it, watch it from the outside looking in, but you can't stop it, you can't change it.

"Where'd you find it?" Jack's voice was dull, his question more a demand than anything.

"Outside Manhattan, Kansas..."

"Outside *where?!*"

Inside a second the collar of my shirt was caught in a firm fist, one that hauled me forward until Jack's hot breath filled my nose.

"Who the fuck told ya you could go to Manhattan? Huh? Answer me, boy!"

But he didn't give me time, instead he shoved me away from him till I hit the floor.

"So not only did you disobey my orders, you endangered the lives of our people for some fool's errand. That's it, ain't it? You were goin' after some shit piece o' doodad for yer fucking portal? Ya ain't no engineer, Sharkey, ya ain't nothin but a disappointment. And to top it off, ya bring back a broken bot. No bullets? No scrap?"

I gritted my teeth, heart racing as I shoved myself back to my feet.

"But I can make it work again, Jack. It ain't fer nothin'. I can fix it! And I can use the safe city chip in its hand to open every damn door on that train! We can get more than we've ever got before, don't you see? But it's more than that, Jack! We can get into Kansas City now! Nothin' can stop me. I'm gonna take my people through the portal if it's the last thing I do."

"'All I see is a kid who ain't done dreamin' and who ain't ready to lead no one. Now there ain't gonna be no train job. I wish them boys never woulda told ya about it…" He trailed off, gray eyes sweeping over my shoulder, seeking out two faces, one of which he would not find. Porter beside me recoiled, her eyes cast down at her worn boots, before she stepped forward. I made note of the fact that one of her shoulders was in front of me now, perhaps to protect me from the fallout she knew was coming.

"Sir, Isaac didn't make it back," she said quietly. "We lost him in Manhattan."

My ears rang. It was all I could hear for a second and I feared I might pass out. The world got dark and my heart raced in my chest. Only Porter's hand on my forearm steadied me, made me realize I was hearing my father screaming at the top of his lungs. I am not really sure what he said. All of it was loud.

Most of it made me out to be little, stupid, nothin' but a piece of shit who wouldn't have known responsibility if it slapped me in my face. Then before I knew it, I was standing outside. It was nighttime, the critters were howling and chirping in the trees, and a warm breeze picked at a couple strands of my red hair. He had gone on to say I wasn't to set foot near that train the next morning, but I had the robot now. There was only one path I could take.

"Lemme guess. You didn't hear shit he just said. Yer still doin' the train job, and uh, it's destiny or some fucking pansy-ass shit like that?" Porter's humored deliverance found my ears before my eyes could make her out in the dark, a smile springing to my lips where once a scowl had been.

"Lemme guess," I countered, humor in my eyes. "Yer coming with me whether I like it or not?"

She laughed, a harsh, quick sound that she made with her nose and the back of her throat. Even then I could tell it was honest.

"You don't give up kid, I will give ya that. But you gotta start thinkin' about the shit that's goin' on down here, cuz whatever's goin' on in there,"—she tapped a finger over my forehead to accentuate her meaning—"it ain't the same. And I won't be able to protect you forever."

I scoffed, ducking my head to escape the leather hat that she proceeded to swat at me. "I don't need you protectin' me, Porter." But I did. And she knew I did too.

We stood there together, shoulders propped against one another's, voices silenced, eyes watching the black Kansas River till the sun made it orange. Then in unison, without talking, without wondering anymore about what we'd do, we seemed to sync. And I didn't have to tell her to get the others.

We saddled our horses without saying much else. Porter was finished first; then she spent the next few minutes helping her wife get tacked up, a gentleness in her hands when she helped Tatiana into her saddle that was reserved for her and her alone. Wes was too busy bothering me to saddle his own horse and had spent the last few minutes smirking at me as he fussed with my saddle bags, cracking wise about my father and various objects he obviously had up his ass. Nadine never showed, and the preacher, well he was on his knees at the stable doors praying, and I listened as the others packed their bags.

"These violent delights have violent ends," the preacher said softly. "And in their triumph die, like fire and powder, which as they kiss consume...."

I don't know whether it was the way the wind picked up when he said that last bit or if it was the way he'd delivered his sermon like it weighed on him. Whatever it was, it made my chest tighten under my shirt.

"He ain't comin' with." Porter spoke softly, eyes cast over toward her kneeling father as he muttered into the dawn.

"I know he wants to go out fightin', but it won't be while I'm watchin'."

I glanced back, gesturing toward Tatiana, who was singing something to her horse and braiding its main. "Yer lettin' Tatiana come?"

Porter snorted, a smirk playing over her lips. "I can boss my old man around, but my wife? I don't think so."

We smiled at each other, a moment settling between us that seemed to have this definite end. We could see it, we could feel it, but neither of us seemed willing to conclude it, both of us knowing that when we did, we would have to face what came next. Eventually the symphony of a waking city made the decision for us, forcing us all onto our mounts and off toward the edge of town. As we rode out, other willing participants joining us here and there, the preacher called out into the dawn from the stable doors.

> "Experience teacheth us
> That resolution's a sole help at need:
> And this, my lord, our honour teacheth us,
> That we be bold in every enterprise:
> Then since there is no way, but fight or die,
> Be resolute, my lord, for victory."

CHAPTER FIVE

RICKY

T HE TOWN WAS QUIET EXCEPT FOR THE RHYTHMIC
sound of an old guitar being strummed somewhere far off.
Smoke rose from a campsite near the riverbank by the old
power plant. Some two hundred years ago, it had been
a bustling alcove that welcomed park visitors toward a running
trail. Now it was overgrown and absent of the masses that had
once traversed it on the squishy heels of tennis shoes.

Ricky Lane sat there on that bank with his back to the town,
broad shoulders set and elbows resting over his knees. The
crackling fire before him hissed, two logs collapsing slowly into
themselves as he watched through half-lidded eyes. Ricky was
a simple man with simple opinions about the world. The others
often described him as somber, but he was a good man to follow
and he always kept them safe no matter what.

Another figure approached from the shallow hill that came
down from the road above them. This man was smaller than
Ricky, his high cheekbones made softer by brown peach fuzz
that he neglected to keep shaved. His blue eyes were quiet, kept
in their place by too many lines. He had his hands tucked in the
pockets of his trousers, though one abandoned the safety of the
secluded dark to brush haphazardly through his mop of dark,
sleep-tousled hair.

Ricky didn't bother to look at who'd come. He knew it was
Kent Watson. It was always Kent who joined him at his camp by
the riverside.

"What the hell ya doin awake before noon?" Ricky smiled, an
expression he rarely used when company was about. Kent didn't
really count as company though. He was around too often for
that. *Company* was a word reserved for long-lost cousins who
would come in the dead of night after a long wagon ride with

bags in hand and too many loud children, none of whose names you knew.

Kent grunted instead of replying directly, fingers rubbing over one of his eyes as he plopped down in the grass beside the fire ring. Their eyes met for a moment, and finally Kent yawned a response.

"Got woken up by a shit-ton o' horses headin' outta town."

Ricky lifted a brow, curiosity piqued. Whatever his hands were busy with, they paused.

"Who was it?"

"Hell if I know." Kent rolled over onto his back, his smaller frame decompressing as he heaved and released a disgruntled sigh. He stared up at the sky for a moment, tracing the huge swath of light pink clouds over toward the horizon where the trees took them. He winced. "All this sun ain't good for me, Ricky." He rolled away from the wretched glow dramatically, one arm hitching over his face to shield it from the minuscule amount of sun the dawn had cast on him. Ricky rolled his eyes, furry jaw clenched as his large hands continued to work at something over the fire.

"Ya ain't a damn bat, Watson, fer fuck's sake." He was still smiling though, blue eyes squinting in concentration. The moment of silence that followed the quip was enough to make Kent glance up curiously from where he lounged.

"I might be," he countered, but he couldn't hide his grin either. "What are you doing, anyways?"

Ricky looked skeptical, like if he said it out loud it would somehow jinx it.

"I uhhh, I am makin' coffee," he said finally, eyes swiveling over toward Kent with some manner of warning in them. The reveal was enough to get the other man to sit up fully, a whistle sounding through his pursed lips as he slapped his hands over his own legs.

"This should be good. You gonna wreck the whole camp when it goes wrong this time?"

"You just watch, Kent. Someday." Suddenly Ricky didn't sound so much like he was kidding, his voice somber and full of yearning. "Someday I'm gonna make the perfect cup of coffee or die tryin'." His rough hands poised so that the pan of boiling water that he held didn't spill as he tipped it over the ground beans and the cloth cover of his mug. Kent watched, trying not to show that he was counting the seconds that passed while it brewed.

After letting it steep, adding the fresh cream and the sugar like they were volatile ingredients being added to a beaker, and staring at it for far too long, it was finally time to taste it. Kent's breath caught in his chest as Ricky lifted his mug slowly to his lips.

There was only one person in the whole world that Kent cared enough about to want happiness for, and that person was Ricky Lane. Now, even after becoming familiar with so many sides of Ricky that weren't as kind as others, if you asked, he wouldn't change a thing.

Ricky cursed under his breath, swallowing with what looked like little satisfaction.

"It ain't perfect," he whispered, voice so broken that it made Kent's chest tighten. Tentatively he reached out a rough hand, clasping it on Ricky's nearest drooping shoulder.

"Hey, someday it will be. And whether we gotta take a boat across the sea to find yer beans or milk a safe city cow, we'll do it." Kent cleared his throat once he finished, hand hesitating briefly before he pulled it away and his weight fell back onto a supportive elbow.

"Now stop mopin' and pour me a cup, won't ya? Hell, I don't care if it tastes like battery acid, long as it works." He smiled, and even though he wasn't in the mood, Ricky did too.

Ricky watched Kent drink his coffee with something like envy in his eyes. That someone could consume it with so little regard for its taste or its essence made him simultaneously sick and jealous.

Together they sat, expressions pensive, eyes gazing out over the mist that rose above the river. Sometimes they'd speak, a joke here, a comment there, and when Ricky's Australian shepherd, Bean, found her way out of the tent and settled at her master's feet, one of his rough hands fell down to stroke the brown fur along her back. It was Kent who broke the last bout of silence that had fallen between them.

"Ya know what I miss?"

"Hm?"

"Autumn."

Ricky snorted, glancing over to fix his companion with a questioning look.

"Kent, ya ain't ever seen autumn. Hasn't been a season like that since the twenty-second century. We weren't even alive."

Kent frowned, shrugging his shoulders as his expression shifted from disappointment to bliss. "Yeah, but there's stories, stories about how it got cold, stories about how the leaves turned yellow and orange, and there's that stupid romance movie they watch down at the Free Place. People would put pumpkins on their porches. There was even this silly holiday where all the kids would dress up like monsters and go runnin' around askin' for sweets or somethin', I dunno what it is. I just wish it would get cold enough to wear cozy sweaters an' snuggle up by the fire...ya know?"

Ricky smiled, glee in his eyes as he reached out to prod Kent playfully.

"Congratulations, Kent. Deep down yer just a twenty-second-century teenage girl."

Bean growled softly, hackles rising to alert her master of an approaching figure. Both men glanced over to see who it was.

"Easy, Bean, it's just Crystal." Ricky watched the girl as she approached, her long brown hair all braided and decorated with flowers that she'd found somewhere. She wasn't smiling like usual, and her sky-blue eyes looked uneasy, nestled beneath long lashes. Her many-beaded bangles and the string of tiny gold bells around her waist made it almost impossible not to notice her, and somehow she'd still managed to sneak up on them.

Crystal Brady claimed to be an empath and a witch just like her mother and her grandmother before her. The thing was, only Ricky really believed her, and he'd fight tooth and nail to make sure she didn't feel ridiculed by his people for the way she saw the world.

So when she stepped up behind him and sat a delicate hand on his shoulder, eyes full of fright, he paid her a particular sort of mind.

"The riders," she whispered, voice small. "Somethin' bad's comin'."

Kent murmured a noise beneath his breath that sounded doubtful, but Ricky knew better. He'd been listening to Crystal's warnings for years, and she'd yet to let him down. It was only seconds that passed between their eyes before another figure had joined them, this one quite recognizable.

"Boys. Crystal. I got word from the guards that my son went tearin' off outta the gates this mornin' with some o' my best scrappers. Ya'll saddle up. We're goin' after him. I got a feelin' he's tryin' that train job. Fuckin' punk." Papa Shark looked rough, old eyes glaring as they swept over the gathered faces. His words had not been posed like a question. It was an order, and without pause, the men had risen, awakened the others, and made their way to the stables.

Ricky and Kent saddled their horses together, side by side, whatever banter they shared hushed as they worked their tack with practiced hands. Kent always whispered things to his gray gelding, Bandit, and Ricky and his palomino, Cow, watched with amusement in their eyes. Mayra joined them soon after. She hardly ever spoke, but her presence alone implied strength and sent most running for cover. She and her Clydesdale, Copper, made their way out first into the yard.

Jon and Clay were the last to rise from their tents, Jon hurrying Clay on and ushering him up toward their stabled mares. Clay's white horse, Abigale, was blind since birth and followed Jon's appaloosa, Star, no matter where she went. It seemed almost poetic to Ricky, as Clay, too, had been born without something. The man had a talent that no other man could ever have, but with the gift he'd been given came a crippling disadvantage. He was a simple man in its simplest meaning, but Jon was always there to protect him and help him grapple with the tasks in life he couldn't handle alone.

"You good, Clay?" Ricky asked, head nodding toward Clay's taller form. The man across from him smiled the widest smile he thought he'd ever seen and one he'd grown quite accustomed to.

"Clay's good, Ricky." He grinned at his feet shyly as Jon worked the blind mare's bit into her mouth for him.

Crystal was the only one whose paint mare still whinnied from her stall.

"Don't worry, Destiny, ya ain't going out with us tonight; you settle down now, girl." Ricky soothed her quietly, though Papa Shark wasted little time as he called out from the street.

"C'mon!" An order that seemed to simultaneously rouse all of them from their pace and double it. Then, with Crystal's cryptic warning stalking his heels, Ricky and the rest of his crew galloped out into the quiet Lawrence streets.

CHAPTER SIX

THE TRAIN JOB

HE AIR FELT THICK WITH FEAR AND THE SMELL OF
grinding metal car wheels on the tracks. I couldn't be
sure how long it had taken us to reach the yard, but
unfortunately the train was already in place, basking in
the warm sun like a huge silver snake. We only counted thirty
soldiers, all armed and spread out around the open car doors.

"We missed our chance. We can't blow through the bottom
like we usually do."

Porter ridiculed my timing from behind my left shoulder, arms
crossed over her chest, uncertainty in her eyes.

"So we find another way." I used the robot's arm as an
extension of my own and gestured awkwardly toward the train
beneath us. The hill we perched on banked down steeply and
opened up into a worn grass clearing cut in half by the tracks
and littered with dilapidated market stalls. This yard was
hardly ever used, and when it was, those stalls were usually only
occupied by innocent farmers unloading their crops.

It wasn't set up for a battle. There wasn't any cover save for
a few old, rusted car shells that had been torn apart by time
and desperate scrappers. I cursed beneath my breath, attention
wavering between the opening and closing train doors guarded
by soldiers and the many faces behind me who waited for
my orders.

"So," I started, craning over the edge of the hill just enough so
that I could see the yard and the first few guards talking among
themselves near the start of the wooded trailhead.

"You guys distract the guards. Start some commotion over
there by the stalls, and I'll take the robot's arm and sneak into
one of the train cars from the other side. Once I'm inside I'll be
able to unlock the doors with the safe city chip." Should I have

told them it was the last train car I needed to get into, the one farthest away? Maybe. With far too much confidence, I nodded firmly and slid down the hill on the heels of my boots toward the train.

▪

I opened my eyes into a harsh white light. I could feel cool concrete beneath my fingers, one pad and the edge of a nail brushing over a sharp crack in the floor. I was in a daze. The air was too thick, and it was difficult to breathe. I tried harder, gasping as pain overcame my body. My nerves figured out that I was still alive and started reacting to the injuries I had sustained.

"Welcome back. Do you remember what happened?" I heard Ricky's voice, but it sounded like it was a million miles away from me.

"Not really." I realized only then how dry my mouth was and coughed instead of continuing. A rough hand offered out a glass of water and I took it greedily.

"Where am I?"

I tried looking around again when my eyes grew accustomed to the light overhead, a bare bulb swaying slightly from the center of the gray ceiling.

Ricky watched me from his perch on a backwards chair, his arms folded casually over the back; and he had a solemn expression on his face.

"The jail," he said, voice cool.

Then I saw the bars and a panic I was not prepared for racked through my chest. The haze that encompassed my head was fading.

"The train job. Wh-what happened?"

"You tell me." Ricky's coaxing was more like an order, and I found myself involuntarily trembling. I wasn't sure if I was scared, but I certainly wasn't cold. Something in the back of my mind stirred, memories surfacing without my say-so.

I remembered careening through the train car with the robot's arm clenched tightly in my hand. One lock down, two, three, there was so much inside, a hundred or so crates of supplies in each car, piled high around me. More food and ammo than I had ever seen. I remembered the bliss that had overcome me, the excitement that had sent adrenaline through my body. Another car was opened. There were no windows available on the walls for me to use to check in on the others. I had three more cars to go until I reached the engine room. There I knew I would find the extension cable I needed to connect the cooling vent in my workshop. That was the reason I pushed so hard for the train job to happen. I hadn't told the others.

I lied to them.

Suddenly I heard gunshots from outside, too many to be accidental or to be warning shots to the others. Fear took hold of me. The cable was in sight. I yanked it unceremoniously from its port within the engine's base, knowing that it would simultaneously prevent the train from leaving before we had unloaded it and facilitate my own project's success.

Then I swung down into the landing where the door was, reached for my holstered weapon, and pushed out into the daylight and the warm wall of air behind it.

"No," I mouthed, unable to determine exactly what I was witnessing.

There were bodies on the ground in pools of carmine blood. Most of them were still alive, if only barely. And I recognized every single one of them. All of them were scrappers from my town. I knew their names: Johny, Karra, Oswald, Jeff. Others were still fighting. Ricky was there, one arm slung around Kent's chest, holding closed a gunshot wound. The soldiers were too many, though. Where had they come from? There had only been thirty. They couldn't have all been on the train.

Another figure approached, the sound of his horse's hooves pounding the ground drawing my attention.

"Get on the damn horse, boy!"

I recognized the deep lines in his forehead. My father loomed over me, rifle in one hand, the reins of his horse in the other.

He yelled again as machine gun fire filled the air. "Get on the fuckin' horse!"

I complied, but something fell from my pocket as I threw my leg over the back of the saddle pad. Gunshots ricocheted around us, screams filled the short expanse of air between me and my father's face. I turned to him, panic rushing through me once more, and before he could stop me, I pushed off and landed haphazardly on the ground. I grabbed the cable that had fallen with struggling fingers, adrenaline forcing my heart into overdrive as I turned back.

That's when the final few shots rang out, *pop pop pop*...then silence. I was confused by what happened next. Everything was blurry, and all that I could see was my father's horse falling toward me. The weight of her knocked the breath out of me, and I went down with her screaming body on top of me. I lost sight of my father, searching for him desperately as I shoved against the whole of sixteen hundred pounds of animal. Her fur was soaked with blood, and as I pushed with my knees and elbows, she took a final staggering breath, wailing in pain.

I couldn't breathe. The world got darker and darker. Someone yelled my name, and then I was back in that cold cell, Ricky staring at me through the tarnished bars.

"I remember..."

■

Mist settled over the city of Lawrence, curling over the damp ground, lapping at the edges of the churning river. It tasted like ash. I stood in that fog with my hands at my sides, my chin turned down toward the ground, and my back against the railing of the Free Place's porch.

Before me, as the morning fog made way for early bands of sunlight and the calls of birds began, my people gathered. Ricky stood with me, a toothpick clutched in his molars, his leather-clad arms folded at his stomach, and a grimace accentuating the lines in his face.

"You gonna be the one who does it?" I asked, my voice softer

than I'd meant it to be. He didn't turn to meet my gaze, though
I watched his dark brown eyes flicker sideways under the rim of
his hat.

"Ain't my job."

"Do you wish it was?"

"Now that's another question, entirely." His expression made
him look even older than he was and more frightening than he'd
been before. I didn't like that look very much.

A wind picked up, blowing the smell of a storm in from the
north and drawing my eyes up toward the rising sun. I hoped to
catch sight of it. I loved storms, the feeling that got caught in my
chest when the temperature dropped, the smell of the rain, the
thunder, and the lightning that often accompanied them. Only
this morning, I didn't love storms any longer.

The crowd divided slowly, mumbling words exchanged
as shoulders brushed and hats were swept from heads. Then
Mama's there, but she looked like a stranger to me. Her face was
different. Pale. Broken. Her eyes, once full of light and love, were
hollow, and even her hair, normally a beautiful orange was dull.
I believed that was the way I would always remember her, and it
was that thought that scared me more than any other.

She stared at me, I stared back, and yet our eyes never met.

"Mama..." I whispered, a question in my voice that I wasn't
sure I wanted answered.

I allowed my eyes to focus on nothing, the world blurring
around me as her expression broke, tears streaming down her
rosy cheeks. I wanted to fight, I wanted to scream, I wanted to
beg her not to, but when I opened my mouth nothing came out
but a sob.

It didn't matter, not when Porter shoved her way through the
crowd. Her voice sounded off like the crack of a whip, making
the muscles in my jaw clench and my eyes widen.

"How dare you?" Before anyone could react, she slapped
Mama right across her face. A gasp echoed through the crowd,
every face turning to watch Ricky and Kent charge forward.

Porter didn't spook, shoulders braced as the boys grabbed her arms and forced her down onto her knees.

"Porter, stop, please! You got a good thing goin' here. Don't throw that away for me, of all people." My voice was a plea, and she looked up under the brim of her hat, her blond, wispy bangs freed from the long braid over her chest, frayed and disheveled.

"I made a promise to your father, Sharkey. You remember the story I told you? Bout the night you were born? I was just a little girl, but he handed you to me that mornin', all bundled up in an old towel, and he made me promise him that I'd always keep you safe. Said you was my responsibility now."

I could hear Mama's sobs, and I found myself on my knees in the street, my hands reaching out for her. All I wanted in the world was my mother to hold me, and I was overtaken by a fear that I had never had before. I would never experience that comfort ever again.

"Please, Mama," I choked, grabbing at her skirts like I used to do when I was little.

"I don't wanna go…"

Porter watched me while Ricky held her in place in the street. Kent couldn't bear to look at me. Mama couldn't seem to meet my eyes either. When she spoke, her voice trembled, and tears streamed down her cheeks, cutting through her blush and drawing it down over her chin.

"Cortez Sharkey," She announced, and it was then that my heart dropped into the pit of my soured stomach. She had never called me Cortez. And I knew in that moment that this was no longer my home.

"I'm here today to have you answer for your crimes. And so to make this quick, so the scrappers can get back to work, I, Luciana Sharkey, leader of Lawrence, sentence you to exile for the crimes of disobeying your leader and goin' on with an assault that ultimately brought on the…the death of over a dozen of your people, including my husband and prior leader of Lawrence, Jack Sharkey. You'll be escorted to the blockade at the bridge, and you'll vow to me this day never to return to this town. Is this sentence clear?"

It must have been a dream, right? Surely none of it was real. The air felt real though, the storm smelled real, the horses sounded real, my mother looked real. The pain in her eyes, that was real.

"It's clear," I mouthed, unable to summon much of a voice.

She nodded once, a quick, robotic gesture, "You'll be given your pony and enough supplies to last you a week. Anyone who wishes to stay with you shall too accept the sentence you've been given and must too vow never to return to this city. Is this clear?"

I didn't understand why I wasn't losing it. I tried, but instead of welling with emotion, I felt…nothing. I thought of my father, slain at the tracks, and I felt nothing. I thought of my mother, standing there, telling me I could never come home, and I felt nothing. So was I broken? And most importantly, could I be fixed?

I turned away from her, not bothering to reply, and I began to walk toward the stables where my pony was being readied for me. The people—*my* people—divided, but in a fashion I was not accustomed to. Many sneered, some cursed at me. One woman rounded on me, and a quick palm found my cheek. I stumbled back, finding her tear-filled eyes in the dewy light.

"You bastard, you killed my husband!" She wailed, and without furthering her attack, left, storming into the distance.

No, I thought to myself, no one could be fixed from this.

Suddenly a figure approached me from my left, shoving people out of the way to get to me. I braced for another impact, and yet received only a gripping hand on my shoulder.

"So, boss, where are we goin'?" Porter barked.

I looked to her, searching her fierce eyes for proof of falsehoods but found only strength there, only conviction, and gratitude, and an emotion I couldn't identify.

I shook my head. "You know they won't let you come back. It'll be dangerous. Hell, we probably won't make it far."

She snorted, the hand cupped over my shoulder gripping me tightly.

"Shut up," she said, moving around me toward the other stabled horses. Not a second later, Tatiana followed after her, and the preacher too. I glanced over my shoulder, searching the crowd for others.

"Lookin for me?" A cocky, youthful voice found me, and Wes popped up to my right, one shoulder leaned against the barn's half-open door. He had a smile on his face, and his young eyes were shrouded in mischief.

"Well, actually," I countered, returning the grin he offered me. "I was lookin' for my robot, but I reckon you'll do." He didn't laugh, but he knew what I meant. He nodded his head toward his horse, still in its stall, my robot tied over its back.

It was the next pair who showed that I wasn't expecting, a woman whose name I couldn't remember for the life of me, making her way through the crowd with a blond boy on her hip. She stopped several feet from me, a look in her eye like she might be spooked any minute and run. I recognized her though, with her yellow hair done up in ribbons and a light blue dress on. I placed her many times before, lined up on the upper balcony of the Free Place with the other upstairs ladies. It's shameful, but at the time I couldn't remember if I had ever slept with her.

"Y-you don't know me, but my name's Peggie Clem, and this here's my son Chesser an', well, we'd like to come with you. I know I ain't strong like the others, but I can cook. I don't wanna die in this town. I want my son to get ta grow old with me."

Her boy smiled from her side, small hands clutched around her shoulders, bright eyes watching me without a care in the world. I nodded to her and watched as the rest of the crowd began to disperse. The sun was high enough now that the scrappers could work, and the exile of Papa Shark's son wasn't worth losing scrap over.

Slowly, the others mounted and gathered beside my pony and me. Porter and Tatiana rode double, Tatiana's arms laced around her wife's middle, the preacher sitting tall, his book of God's words under his arm, Peggie on her mare with her son half asleep against her chest, small hands clutching the mane of their mount. Then Wes, whose charming face seemed ever bright and careless, perched up on his horse's back with an apple and a knife in his hand, stray bangs over his giddy green eyes.

I couldn't help but catch sight of my shed on our way out, and perhaps I had stared at it just a little too long.

Wes saw me, following my gaze and furrowing his brow as he pulled his reins up.

"Hey, what's in there anyways? It's not like you'll ever see it again." One hand brushed his long bangs from his face. I hesitated briefly, though he was right. I'd never see that shed again, so it didn't really matter who knew what was in it.

"I was tryna build my own portal...with a book I found a long time ago...one of them instruction books...." I laughed quietly, a note of self-deprecation on my breath.

"Hell...I didn't get too far. That's why I wanted to do the train job so bad. There was a part that I needed. My backup plan was to take everyone through the portal in Kansas City."

Wes watched me, eyes wide, mouth set.

"And did you find it? The part you needed?"

"Yeah, I did."

"So...where are we going, boss?" Wes hitched his shoulders up a bit, nodding toward the road ahead of us as the others waited. I hesitated again, looking out over the streets of Lawrence one last time before I turned my back on the town.

"Kansas City," I said finally, nodding firmly and kicking my horse up into a gallop that the others followed.

The preacher drowned out the silence that accumulated between us:

> Who alone suffers, suffers most i' th' mind,
> Leaving free things and happy shows behind.
> But then the mind much sufferance doth o'erskip
> When grief hath mates, and bearing fellowship.

CHAPTER SEVEN

THE PYRES

WHAT?" RICKY WATCHED KENT WITH QUIET curiosity and perhaps a hint of accusation in his eyes.

"I didn't say nothin'" Kent replied, shoulders tucked in, arms folded over his chest, back firmly against the tree behind him. The river listened, babbling gently to itself like a young child.

The only light was the crackling fire that sat between them, lapping toward the edges of Ricky's worn leather boots and dancing in the watchful eyes of the dog who lay at her master's feet.

Ricky huffed. "You don't have to say nothin'. I know ya better than that. What? Say it. You know I don't like my people keepin' shit from me, especially you." He glanced up at him, molars gnawing on the strip of jerky that he'd fed into his mouth. Kent looked back, the only man undeterred by those fierce eyes.

"I just think...maybe Mama was a little hard on the kid. That's all."

Ricky snarled, hands bracing over his knees. "So, what? She shoulda just let him off with a smack on the hand? He ain't a kid no more. He got the old man killed, and a lot o' other good people too."

Kent sucked in a short breath, waiting to release it until he could do so with the utmost dramatic flair.

"You're talkin' like you gave a shit about him."

"Don't matter. He was still our leader, and Sharkey still got him killed. Hell, he almost got you killed too, and that means more to me." Ricky gestured toward the bound wound in Kent's side, and Kent shrugged his jacket over it. He didn't reply, only pushed off the tree and plopped down so they faced each other, flames dancing between them. A log popped, and somewhere in the darkness, footsteps approached.

Both men looked up as Crystal appeared, the frills of her tawny skirts clutched up in both her hands so they didn't drag through the mud. She was barefoot, and her melodic voice carried through the night like the song of a siren.

"Boys."

"Crystal."

Her eyes reflected the flames and Ricky's hard face.

"The ceremony's soon. Mama wants you and the others in the Free Place before it starts." She tried to smile, and one small hand rested briefly on Ricky's shoulder. Ricky nodded, grunting quietly under his breath and bringing Kent to his feet with nothing more than a look.

He paused and turned to Kent, one worn hand tapping against the smaller man's chest to get his attention. "Hey," he said, looking him in the eye under the brim of his dark leather hat.

"You and I are still havin' words later, okay?"

Kent returned his boss's stare, though they walked together side by side back up the moonlit hill, across the old rusted train tracks, and up Mass Street toward the brewery's porch in silence.

Already people were gathered in the streets, and the wagon of bodies pulled by two big working horses could be seen between the many shifting faces. Torches were lit and passed out among the townspeople. And even outsiders from the edge of Lawrence and strangers from the farmlands across the bridge had come to bid their farewells. Ricky glanced over them briefly before stepping inside.

The brewery was quieter than usual, and the only person inside was Mama, sitting alone in Papa's chair at the long table. As Ricky and the others approached, she lifted her head, and her tired eyes danced over them.

"Come on over and sit down," she ordered, voice weak and quiet. Ricky did so, though instead of sitting, he stood behind the seat opposite her, and his people followed suit. He looked at the dark circles under her eyes, which no longer held that jovial quality they had before.

Her hands rested over the table, one finger slowly turning the wedding band she still wore.

"I have a task for ya, and ya ain't gonna like it, but it's important to me, you understand?"

Ricky lifts a brow, eyes narrowing.

"Whatever you need, Mama." He bowed his head to her slightly. Mama had always been there to look out for her boys, and Ricky was one of them. She'd raised him herself, and Kent too. Hell, she was the only mama Ricky had ever known. Both men stood together before her, shoulders braced, stance wide and guarded, hands clutched behind or in front of them respectfully. Ricky had even swiped the dark leather hat from his head, and he held it below his belt. Bean sat obediently at her master's side, whining softly after too much quiet had passed.

"Oh c'mere, Bean, old girl," Mama called. She clapped, and Bean rushed forward from her heel, gentle face held in Mama's hands as her tail wagged faster.

Ricky watched, the hint of a smile finding his grizzled face and disturbing the stubble around his mouth.

Then the moment had passed, and Mama stood from her seat, a gentle sigh escaping her as she rounded the table to face them.

"Listen, boys, I know it may not make much sense to you, seeing what y'all just saw me do, but my baby's out there all alone, and I can't live with that unless I know he gets to where he's goin' safe. You understand?"

Ricky waited for the meaning of her words to settle in, but it didn't, and he hesitated, glancing over to see if Kent had figured it out first.

Kent shrugged.

"Um, no, actually, Mama. What are you tryin' to say?"

Mama sighed, glancing toward the door like she was afraid someone might hear.

When she spoke again, her voice was low.

"I need you to follow him, Ricky. Tail 'im till he gets to where he's goin', and you make sure he's safe no matter what."

The color in Ricky's face drained, stubble turning around the scowl that drew over his scarred lips.

"Fuck no." He bit the words off, turning away only to have Mama's hand grasp his arm.

"I wasn't askin'," she said, venom in her voice that the others had never heard before.

"My husband's dead. My friends are dead. My son, my only son...is out there somewhere in The Nothin'...and you, my right-hand fuckin' man, are gonna go out there and make sure he stays alive. You understand me now?"

Kent watched with bewilderment in his eyes, and the second Mama relinquished her grasp on Ricky's arm, a tension shifted between them all. Kent and Bean waited for hell to break loose. It didn't. Instead, miraculously, something like understanding flickered through Ricky's dark eyes, the lines that kept them under thin lashes softening.

"Fine," he replied. He shrugged it off, like the burden was a physical cloak over his shoulders that he wished to cast down onto the old floor.

Mama nodded firmly, and with a last, somber sort of glance back toward the long table, toward the tall-backed chair that Papa used to sit in, she divided them, and moved out through the door and into the amassing crowd outside.

■

The funeral pyres sat checkered over the prairie, dark shapes amongst the pale ryegrass. They didn't belong there, everyone could tell. Kent looked them over, each one smaller than the other as they drifted out of sight, on and on until he could see only blurry hints of them in the distance.

"A man should never see so many in his life," he said, and Ricky watched him with hooded eyes.

"I know...the last I saw so many was the war."

Mama stood with her head bowed so low that her red hair fell around her face and shoulders, stray hairs plastered to her pale cheeks. As the crowd gathered beside them in the field, she took up her skirts from her knees, stood, and reached for the carved goblet she'd set down beside her.

A hush fell over the crowd, and when she spoke, not a single breath was taken that might disturb her words.

"Our preacher isn't here this day, so I'll say my own words to honor our dead. Many have been taken from us, and many shall return this night to The Nothing. May their gods and goddesses accept them with open arms, and may they know that each and every one of them died a warrior's death."

Ricky took a deep breath, waited for Mama to say her piece, then without a word to his crew, he gathered them up at his side. He turned on the heels of his boots, and the lot made off back toward town together with a new and foreboding task to accomplish.

CHAPTER EIGHT

THE LIONS CALL

WHERE WE GOIN', MAMA?" CHESSER HUFFED AND rested his head back against his mother's chest. She ran slender fingers through his hair. She was a dancer before she came with me. The boy smiled, though you could see the tireless coils of energy that all children suffer through building inside his eyes, preparing to burst out.

"The safe city, baby. Can we stop for a bit, Sharkey?" his mother asked, her gentle voice caressing the stormy air. I shook my head, glancing back toward the others.

"We'll make camp soon. Just a few more miles." I looked over their faces again, Porter joining me as we rode.

"I didn't see Nadine," I said quietly, assuming he had been ashamed of me for all the things that I had done that had hurt him: Manhattan, the train job, his brother's death.

Porter tensed, her mount slowing, thinking she meant for him to stop. The horse blew air through his nose, head tossed up as she moved him forward again.

"You didn't hear?" she winced slightly.

I watched her carefully. I dreaded those words anymore.

"Nadine. He killed himself last night. Didn't leave a note."

The wind howled, and we rode on in silence.

■

The gods were punishing me, right? Right. Maybe I had been cursed. Maybe It was karma, something I had done in a past life. I couldn't be sure. All I knew was everything was going to hell.

Porter and Tatiana rode with me for the rest of the journey. Tatiana smiled at me, her kind eyes wide and full of love. At one point she reached for my hand, holding it tightly before releasing it again. I was more thankful for that brief contact than I could have ever said.

Instead, I made sure to try to smile back at her.

It happened quickly, as it usually does. One moment he was this animated, jovial child clapping his hands and babbling into the night. The next hour he was quiet, and the one after that he started to cough. For a few more hours we rode through it, comforting the child as best we could with warm arms, wide smiles, and the few medical supplies that we had with us. But it didn't get better.

Then he was having trouble breathing, coughing into the dark so loudly and so often that the whole group agreed to stop for another night and ride into Kansas City the next day. Nobody said anything, but we all knew that ever since the pandemic, nobody who was sick was allowed inside a safe city. Then something happened, something that none of us had been prepared for. When we woke up, we found fresh lion tracks outside our camp. The lions had known that the boy was going to die before we did, but as I gazed down into those deep, cavernous indentions in the earth, I knew too.

"How can you even say that? No! No! I won't leave him! Never!" Peggie screamed, tears streaming down her rosy cheeks. Guilt spiked through my chest, resting in the pit of my stomach like rotting food. I looked away, though I saw the boy now, watching me through red, swollen eyes.

"I have a duty to these people, Peggie. Their lives are in my hands. There's no way that they will let him into Kansas City. We can't go back and we can't stay out here." My voice shook, and I turned away from her.

She grabbed my jacket, holding on to me, weak from exhaustion.

I pulled hard, leaving her behind on her knees as I approached my pony. Porter watched me, jaw tight, eyes fierce; but she knew I was making the right decision.

"Maybe there's a town," Tatiana said, hopeful. But there wasn't time. I shook my head, clutching at my saddle, back bent,

head resting against firm leather so that my hat tilted down to
reveal messy red hair.

"It's too much of a risk. If he gets the rest of us sick they won't
let none of us through those gates. You think those lions care
which one of us they get? Whether it's the boy or the old man?"
On that day, I made a decision that my soul would never forgive
me for.

"If she won't leave the boy, we've gotta leave them both."
My voice sounded very far away as I spoke, as if I had called
it from a cliff and stood listening far beneath the edge. With
numb fingers, I had taken from my saddle bag a small silver gun,
counted its bullets, and handed it over to her slowly. She took it,
held it to her chest, and sobbed.

"What the fuck, Sharkey. Are you kidding me?" It was
Tatiana's voice again that shook me to my core. I had never heard
her curse before, and I don't think any of us had ever heard such
anger in her sweet voice. I couldn't bear to look at her, but she
insisted, grabbing my chin in her dark hands and pulling my
face around.

"You listen to me, boy. I love you, and I loved your father, and
I love your Mama, but if you leave that little boy to die by lions
and his Mama to watch, I won't ever forgive you." I stared hard
into her big, tearful eyes and turned away.

Peggie watched us, and Chesser watched his mother, unable
to comprehend her suffering. He did not know. He could not
understand. I had never respected someone so much in my entire
life as I respected Peggie Clem that day.

No one spoke as we mounted our horses and set off slowly
toward the city.

We didn't make it far. Tatiana wouldn't allow us to ride into
the city. She insisted that we stop once we had a vantage point
where we could see the wall, sure that with the pistol I had left
Peggie, she would somehow survive and come stumbling into our
camp. Tatiana and Porter stayed quiet in each other's arms, Wes

joked to hide his fear, and the preacher hummed something old beneath his breath.

■

Peggie was raised by two prostitutes upstairs of the Free Place—a woman named Lavender and one they called Aberdine. She had no memory of her parents. She was never taught to read or write or how to count to one hundred. She didn't need any of those skills to do what they did. However, Peggie would always say that if there was one thing she had done right in her whole life, it was Chesser. Chesser was born one stormy night after she labored for thirteen hours. It was not an easy birth, but Peggie would say later that it was the most beautiful thirteen hours she would ever endure.

"Shhh, it's okay. I'm here for you okay? You don't need to be afraid," she whispered, staggered words beneath her breath, lips pressed against Chesser's hair. The evening had finally come, turning the horizon a deep crimson as a sliver of moon crept up over the trees. Her back rested against a slab of rock, and she counted each bullet over and over again in her mind. Six, one for Chesser, one for herself, four for the lions. One by one she would place them in her hands, roll them between her fingers, say the number under her breath, then return them to their chamber.

Chesser coughed against his mother, breath wheezing from his lungs, taken in again, coughed back out.

"Shh...shh. We gotta be quiet, baby." She tried to soothe him, bringing the blanket up around his face and holding him tight in her trembling arms. She tried desperately to start a fire, but it was raining by then. Her fingers shook as she tried the lighter again, watching the flame flicker away through squinting eyes.

"Cold, Mama," Chesser said. He choked, gasping for a breath as tears rolled down his rosy cheeks. Something stirred the pampas grass, drawing tall shadows over the ground before her, and on soft paws, eight lionesses slinked silently forward, revealing themselves without breaking their formation.

Peggie looked up, eyes wide beneath her mess of bangs, her arm tightening around Chesser's body. The lions watched her, all eight of them unmoving and unconcerned about the pistol the woman brandished. They could have waited all night. Eventually the boy would die and they could work together to tear him out of the arms of his pleading mother. However, on this night, they were particularly hungry, and although they were patient creatures, they knew that together, not even that pistol could stop them all.

One lioness stepped forward, her golden eyes half lidded, reflecting in the night. She walked toward the trembling barrel of the gun. A sudden shot sent birds into the air and the lion leaped back, convulsed, then fell still. The others tensed, watching the display cautiously. Another shot rang out, wasted.

"You won't get my baby!" Peggie screamed, no longer concerned with staying quiet to keep the beasts from finding them. Another lioness leaped back, wounded, into the grasses. Another shot missed. A lioness yowled angrily, finally moved by the show. More shots. Then suddenly, silence. The lions circled, pacing on quiet paws. One still cried out in pain from a gunshot that had missed her vital organs entirely, leaving her to die slowly upon the damp earth. The gun clicked, chamber empty, Peggie cried and Chesser wheezed in his mother's arms. He didn't understand what was happening.

The remaining lions stepped forward and without pause one leaped. She grabbed Chesser from his mother's arms with powerful talons, taking him into her jaws. Peggie screamed, kicking, flailing, and fighting against slashing claws and hind legs that were much too strong. She fell backward as Chesser was pulled away. His guttural screams echoed out into the dark, and she fell, bleeding, onto her stomach, one arm extended toward him, reaching.

"Mama!" Chesser called, as the lion above him drove her fangs into his throat. Peggie heard the snap of his neck, his cough-ridden sobs ceased. And as three others turned for her, she watched, eyes unable to close, head lolled back against the blood-soaked soil, as her child was ripped apart.

Somewhere in the dark, Sharkey turned his pony around, hat clutched up against his chest, prepared to tuck it back over his head and ride back the way they'd come as he heard the shots. He counted them. Everyone counted them…one…two…three…four…five…six. Sharkey stared into the dark, listening to the sudden quiet that seemed so unnatural, and then, as the others gathered and the preacher held his face in his hands, Peggie's screams echoed through the ravine.

Tatiana fell to her knees, caught in Porter's arms as tears streamed down her face. Wes looked away, ashamed of his grief. The preacher muttered deep words into the shadows, and Sharkey looked out into the empty night.

> Like as the waves make towards the pebbl'd shore,
> So do our minutes hasten to their end;
> Each changing place with that which goes before,
> In sequent toil all forwards do contend.

CHAPTER NINE

DIGGING GRAVES

T HE NIGHT WAS FULL OF NOISES, WHISPERS THROUGH the trees, paw pads of curious animals rustling through the underbrush, and horses shaking the metal fastenings of their bridles. However there was one sound that Ricky heard on the breeze that haunted him, something that pulled at his mind and tortured his thoughts. *Click, click, click.*

"Oh would ya just sit down? Ya gotta eat somethin', Ricky. Who cares about some sound in the forest? I don't hear shit."

Kent watched him with concern in his eyes, and a bowl of beans held up on one palm. Ricky shrugged him off, pacing back toward the shadowy tree line with his hand on his pistol and something wild in his eyes.

"Oh, what?" Kent called, scoffing.

"You gonna shoot the scary noise? Hell, Ricky, I've never seen you like this."

Ricky turned on a heel, hand slowly raising from the hilt of his gun and shoved into an armpit resentfully.

"Lay off me," he growled, shuffling toward the fire and plopping down with exaggerated movements.

Crystal smiled, reaching for Ricky's hand and curling ring-covered fingers over the rough skin of his knuckles. "There's something in the air, Ricky." Her quiet voice was fragile, like the wind in the tall grass. "I sense it too...pain...great pain."

Ricky watched her with the same serious look in his eyes that he always had when she spoke of the future. Where Kent shook his head across the fire, Ricky never looked away, brow furrowed, jaw set, completely enthralled with what she had told him and that sparkle of mystery in her wide blue eyes.

Before Kent could open his mouth again, Mayra's huge hand appeared at Ricky's side, a bowl of beans once again thrust toward her leader's chest. This time *no* was apparently not an option.

"Eat," Mayra snapped, her thick voice drawing looks of surprise from those gathered around the fire. Even Clay gawked, all of them waiting for Ricky to shove the bowl away and turn his nose up at the gesture. Instead Ricky took that bowl of beans without argument and spooned some into his mouth with what looked like only mild resentment.

Kent rolled his eyes.

"Unbelievable. You know the beans that *I* offered you were seasoned special, right? Used the last packet of pepper I had and everything." Ricky smirked just to tempt him into a quarrel, and Kent got to his feet, waving him off as he lumbered toward his tent.

"Fuck off," he called, trailing a single finger behind him. Ricky watched as Bean got up and followed him, waiting for the distant "Well, at least the *dog* loves me!" before he laughed through his nose. Slowly, one by one, the others retreated into their tents as well, Mayra offering only a grunt and a nod, Jon giving a gentle wave as he corralled Clay toward his bed, and Crystal pressing a loving kiss to Ricky's forehead. Then at last Ricky sat alone, staring down into the crackling coals that crumbled into plumes of smoke.

The night lulled on, the crickets chirping, the trees rustling, the fire hissing. But that noise never let up, continuing for more than an hour. Finally, deciding he could take the noise no more, Ricky shoved himself to his feet, grabbed his holstered gun from the stump beside him, and headed off alone into the forest. Not long after he started into the shadows, Bean joined him, her paw pads soft against the cushioned bed of decaying plant matter beneath her. Ricky hushed her softly, peering through the dark as the clicking went on and on, growing louder and louder.

Suddenly Bean barked, snarling and growling as she took off through the underbrush.

"*Bean!*" Ricky cursed under his breath as he followed after her, charging forward through branches and bushes. He could hear her still, her raucous voice growing louder as he stumbled out into a clearing, the open field fading off into thick prairie grass taller than his knees. A huge rock formation stood before him now; and, just barely, he could see Bean on the other side. He lunged forward, pistol drawn as he rounded the corner.

The smell of death came first, and then before him lay a sight he would never forget. Crimson blood littered the ground, smeared over the bodies of several slain lions that Bean sniffed and nosed at. The lions' tracks led off, more blood pooled in the indents of their paws in the bare ground. But there was more. Lying there between the bodies of lions was another. This one belonged to a human boy—or it had, before. Now it was merely scraps, and what remained was almost unidentifiable. From his left, that sound... *click, click, click*. Ricky turned toward it, his pulse quick, his eyes wide as he stared into the face of a young woman.

She lay with her back against the rock, her eyes bloodshot and unblinking, her stomach ripped open so her guts poured out over her legs. And in her hand, she still clutched the gun she'd been given, trembling fingers pulling the trigger over and over again. *Click, click, click.*

Ricky stood in the aftermath of that horrendous night, eyes steely. He had seen worse things, people killed, tortured. He had endured hell and had the people he loved taken from him in horrible ways. And still, his stomach turned at the sight. It took him minutes to react, to move forward, knees colliding with the firm earth, hands reaching to steady her, to take the gun, for palms to press against her rosy cheeks. He had to pry the pistol from her stiff fingers, and he set it in the dirt beside them.

"P-peggie?" He recognized her now, her rouged lips, the shape of her cheeks.

"Oh god, Peggie...is...is that *Chesser*?"

Peggie's eyes rolled up beneath her painted lids, her body convulsing. She gasped, blood bubbling over her lips, carving tracks along her porcelain skin. Ricky knew exactly what had to be done, and in one swift motion, with a gentleness he showed only to his dog, he scooped her up into his arms, laid her head gingerly against his shoulder, and he held her. An hour passed or more, while the sun rose slowly, turning the tall grass golden, and Ricky sang softly beneath his breath.

Then, as Bean wagged her tail, nose against the open palm that lay across Ricky's lap, he pressed the barrel of his gun against Peggie's corn-yellow hair and pulled the trigger.

■

Ricky stepped into the campsite with a weight on his shoulders he hadn't felt in a long time. Bean watched him, her dark eyes wide as she crossed behind him and ducked into Kent's tent. Ricky followed her, pulling open the canvas door and staring down at the man half out of his sleeping bag, one arm stretched over his face. For a moment, he debated whether to wake him. Bean curled up at his side. He listened to his familiar snore and his gentle voice in the shadows. Perhaps it would be better if he just let them all sleep, if he spared them from the horror that lay beyond those woods.

"That's really fuckin creepy, Ricky," Kent mumbled from the floor, one hand shielding his face from the tongue of the dog who had woken him, her tail wagging, her gentle whine the only noise now.

"Ricky?" Kent's voice changed.

Ricky glanced away, hands balled into fists as he nodded behind him. "I uh…I need your help. Jon's too. We've got some graves to dig, okay?"

Kent stared, brows raising, frown pulling at the corners of his lips. He nodded, pushing himself up and pulling his coat over his shoulders.

"Okay, Ricky," he said softly, not daring to question him that night. One hand clutched the taller man's shoulder as they turned away and ducked back into the clearing.

Crystal had woken now, and she stood watching him at the entrance of her tent, a pastel blanket pulled tightly around her small shoulders.

"You found the pain," she whispered.

Ricky crossed toward Jon and Clayton's tent. Crystal joined Kent, who shrugged and muttered confused responses to her quiet questions.

"Mayra, the camp's yours. Keep them safe. We'll be back." Ricky made sure to give Crystal a reassuring sort of look as he turned his back on them, but the expression never really made it to his eyes.

Both Kent and Jon walked at Ricky's side obediently, shovels clutched in their hands, still rubbing sleep from their eyes as rays of sunlight crept slowly through the forest canopy. Emerald leaves made the light turn green, and when the wind came up from the prairies on the other side of the forest, the branches bent and moaned quiet protests.

"Ricky?" Kent had stepped up to Ricky's shoulder, and there was something hard in his gaze, a look that Ricky had only seen in Kent's eyes during wartime. Ricky shook his head. Something silent passed between them with that little turn of his lips, a tilt of his head, a line that appeared on his brow as he nodded off toward the rock in the distance. Kent dropped his shoulders, moving forward with a weariness that was obvious in the careful steps that he took.

"Fucking hell." Jon said. He turned away from the mutilated body of the child half scattered over the damp earth.

Kent's expression shifted, some manner of mask forming on his face, and his blue eyes set on Peggie with too much familiarity in their backs. This was not the first time these men had seen such brutality, and it would not be the last.

"She left with Sharkey. She...they were with Sharkey."

"I know." Ricky and Kent's eyes met as the golden sun broke through the clouds and flooded the scene with amber light.

Kent braced himself against the boulder, eyes closed, head resting back against the cool rock. He stared a little too long at the hollow in Peggie's head, knowing what Ricky had been forced to do.

"How could Sharkey just leave them? I don't understand. The kid. He was supposed to take care of them. Do you think the lions got him too? What about Porter and the others?"

Ricky reached out, clasping a hand on Kent's shoulder and tugging him forward into a hug that surprised even Jon, who had reappeared to face the carnage around them. Kent hesitated, unfamiliar with the gesture of condolence that Ricky was displaying but not opposed to it. After a moment, he clapped a firm hand over Ricky's back and as quickly as it had begun, the display was over and the two parted, meeting eyes briefly.

"Who do you think his father was?" Kent asked softly, unable to look at the boy directly as they worked their shovels into the prairie grass. Ricky paused, turning something over in his hand that he had found beside the boy's remains. A toy car, worn by grubby fingers and caked with blood.

Ricky had given the car to Peggie after Chesser was born, sure that the boy was his and desperate to be a part of his life. She had never given him the opportunity.

"You?" Kent asked Ricky.

"Jon?"

Both men exchange a look, shoulders shrugging slightly as they haul the dirt up, tossing it behind them, digging deeper.

"Maybe," Ricky trailed off as if the concept was too much to comprehend.

"Nobody's his father now. He's dead. Don't matter."

Kent paused, expression almost disappointed as he watched Ricky work.

"It matters," he snapped, looking away and out into the rising sun that hung over the horizon now.

It took hours to dig the grave, to lift the bodies, what was left of them, into the pit, and cover them. It took seconds to say their words and minutes to return to the camp, sweaty, sad, and covered in blood-soaked soil. As Mayra, Crystal, and Clay watched over sizzling eggs and the smoke from the morning fire, nobody asked any questions. They had been digging graves. Nothing else needed to be said.

CHAPTER TEN

KANSAS CITY

THINK THEY COULD HAVE FORGIVEN ME FOR ISAAC. I think they could have forgiven me for my father and for the other scrappers who died during the train job, but I don't think they ever really forgave me for Peggie and Chesser. I knew so by the way they looked at me when they didn't know that I was watching. There was one night, though, the night before we rode into Kansas City, that seemed to restore a little of that hope I clung to.

"You ever love anyone before, Sharkey? Thinkin' back, I can't recall seeing ya with anyone before." It was Porter who spoke, long after the others had crawled into their tents, and only the fire sat between us. Porter stirred it awake with the end of a stick, calling ashes and smoke into the air.

"Course I have." My eyes turned away from her into the dark forest that loomed around us.

"What happened?" She watched me with honest curiosity, and I shrugged my shoulders, one hand running up to swat the hat from my head so I could run a hand through my hair.

"What do you think? I fucked it up."

Porter scoffed, shaking her head and sitting back in her folding chair like she knew somethin' I didn't.

"What?"

"Yer a fuckin' idiot is what."

I rolled my eyes, tucking my hat back over my head so she didn't get to see the heat in my cheeks.

"That girl wouldn't've cared that you were broken, Sharkey. We're all fuckin' broken pieces o' shit. That's what The Nothin' does to you…it sucks everything outta you that you thought you knew, and all ya got left in the end is how to survive. And that's all that you can do, survive one fucking day at a time. That's

why yer an idiot. Cuz all this time you coulda been surviving
with her. What was her name, by the way? The girl." I looked
up, puzzled by her words, the way she said them with so much
certainty but she wasn't looking at me any longer. She was
looking at the tent where Tatiana slept blissfully.

Something occurred to me then that had never occurred to me
before. Porter loved Tatiana more than anything in the world,
and she had trusted me to keep her safe.

"Antonia. Her uh...her name was Antonia. The one who
got away."

After a moment Porter stood, crossed to me, and cupped her
flask into the palm of my hand, one finger and the pad of her
thumb grappling for my earlobe. She yanked it hard enough for
me to swat at her, a grin playing over my lips; and for just those
few seconds, nobody was dead, the jungle was quiet, and I didn't
feel so empty anymore.

■

The next day, we rode over the last hill, and there beneath us,
Kansas City rose up from the earth, gray and endless. It crept
back over the horizon like a disease, the tall towers in its middle
stretching up over the gray, unbreachable wall that guarded it. I
glanced back, watching the sun reflect in the lifeless face of the
robot that hung over Wes's saddle, and with a deep breath and a
nod to my people, we rode on, hooves sliding over gravel, until
we stepped out onto the old road that stretched forward through
the cattle yards.

It was about here the stench hit us, forcing our hands over our
mouths. Death. There was no mistaking that smell.

"Where's that coming from?" Complaints echoed around me
as horses blew air through wide nostrils, hooves clicking over
crumbled road. They wanted nothing to do with whatever was
waiting for us.

I shook my head, eyes cast over the empty fields.

"Somethin's wrong."

I shoved my heels into Buddy's sides, charging forward as fast as I could down that straightaway toward the city gates in the distance. Nothing in that moment mattered but disproving the doubt that riddled my mind; it drove my heart into my throat. This was one of the few times I regretted holding onto Buddy for so long. A horse could have gotten to the end of that run much faster, and a full-size saddle would have kept my legs from chafing against the leather.

The closer we got to Kansas City, the worse the smell became, forcing us all to pull our bandannas over our noses just to breathe. Then we saw them through the last mile: hundreds of thousands of dead cattle strewn haphazardly at the foot of the wall, as if they had been tossed over without care for the other livestock that could still be alive. There was only one reason that the people in that city would ever resort to something so barbaric as risking the lives of their herd with the dead.

I hurried from my saddle, boots hitting the ground hard as hoofbeats thundered over the road behind me.

"Gimme the robot, quick Wes. Help me with it!"

Wes looked lost as he undid the ties holding the thing to the back of his saddle, helping me lower it carefully to the ground.

Porter looked between us, at the heaps of rotting carcasses, back toward the wall, back to me again. She knelt to talk to me, her voice all too knowing for my liking.

"Sharkey, you know damn well you don't wanna open that gate. There's only one reason you throw good food out. They got sick, sick enough to poison the rest of the herd, and whatever happened in there was bad enough that the people inside didn't care."

I didn't reply, shaking my head as I worked open the access panel in the back of the robot's head with my pocket-knife, streams of wires and complicated electrical plates pouring out into my hands.

"How do you know about fixin' their kind, boy?"

Only the preacher's voice was enough to stir me from my work, my tongue pressed between my lips as I looked up to meet his eyes beneath the brim of my hat. I hesitated, glancing between the others.

"I, uh...I found a manual durin' a raid. I spent every night for over ten years sittin' in that shed readin' that book, tryin' to figure out what the hell it meant, and eventually..." I trailed off, the preacher prompting me to continue with the raising of his bushy brows.

I shrugged my shoulders, snapping a plug into a slot that matched.

"Well, I figured it out."

As if on cue, a low hum emanated from the robot, rising quickly to a high, wailing alarm. We clutched hands over our ears and scuttled backward as the robot sat up, pressed its metallic palms to the earth, and stood to face us.

"Warning! You are approaching a quarantined area. For your own safety, turn around immediately! Warning! You are approaching a quarantined area. For your own safety, turn around immediately!" The message continued as I pushed myself up, scraping fingers over the dirty rounds of my knees as I peered up at what could have been our salvation.

"Tell it to stop, Sharkey!" Tatiana looked like she was about to cry, Porter looked like she was about to shoot it, and Wes and the preacher looked like they were about to hightail it in the opposite direction, both of them already mounted on their horses.

"Robot! Robot! *Stop!* Turn the alarm off!" It stopped. I was able to turn and face it. It was taller than me, as tall as Ricky, probably, but thinner, spindly, and its blank face stared at us as tiny lights blinked into existence on its silver chest.

"I...I did it." The others seemed less impressed.

"Quarantine? The fuck happened?" Porter demanded, glancing past the robot as she slid her pistol back into its holster.

I swallowed hard as the robot spoke again, its vacant, computerized voice oddly chipper.

"Four months ago, a contaminated cow was consumed by

the citizens of Kansas City, resulting in a quickly mutating
virus that spread throughout the other livestock and the human
inhabitants. Over 500,000 humans died, and the city was
deemed inoperable and unsafe to enter. After the plague of 2020,
any contaminated city must be quarantined and fully processed
by the CDC before any human may enter or exit the premises
as per Regulation 553. If after that quarantine period, the city
is still contaminated, it will be destroyed to prevent further
infection."

"Holy shit..." Porter's voice drew me from the fugue state I
had entered, but nothing seemed to make any more sense in the
real world I snapped back to.

"Um..." I tried to think as panic enveloped the others.

"What are we gonna do now?" Porter asked, reaching out to
steady the trembling shoulders of Tatiana, who desired nothing
more than to return to Lawrence.

"We can go back...right? I mean...Mama would
understand..."

The preacher scoffed.

> Or if there were a sympathy in choice,
> War, death, or sickness, did lay siege to it,
> Making it momentary as a sound,
> Swift as a shadow, short as any dream,
> Brief as the lightning in the collied night
> That in a spleen unfolds both heaven and earth,
> And ere a man hath power to say "Behold!"
> The jaws of darkness do devour it up.
> So quick bright things come to confusion.

"Hell, I don't even know any other safe cities. Are there any
left?" I cast my eyes toward the horizon as I ask.

The robot replied.

"The nearest functioning safe city is Dallas. Dallas, Texas, is

505.9 miles away. Using a vehicle, it would take you eight hours and three minutes."

Wes snorted, and I fixed him with a displeased look.

"Well, we don't got vehicles. We got horses, and it will take us a hell of a lot longer than eight hours to ride horses that far."

"So? What's the move, boss?" Porter crossed her arms under her breasts.

I turned away, reaching for my pony's reins and swinging up into my saddle. "Well"—I pulled Buddy around so fast that his hooves clattered over the road.—"Mount up. Looks like we're headin' to Dallas."

■

The horses jogged through the prairie, the sun hot on our backs. The robot struggling to keep pace, stumbling hurriedly over the uneven terrain, but it never complained. I wasn't even sure if these things were meant for walking around over hills and through the jungle paths.

I slowed my pony to a walk, and watched the robot as Wes rode up on my left.

"So, robot, tell me a joke."

I rolled my eyes, interjecting, though I already knew it wasn't going to make any difference to that boy.

"It ain't a toy, Wes," but he pulled his horse around so my pony was forced over toward the side of the trail. It was a playful gesture, but Buddy whinnied, side-stepping the larger horse and pulling his lips back as a warning.

The robot tilted its metallic face, the lights along its head and the contours of its human-shaped chest contemplating brightly.

"How do you make a hankie dance?" it asked after a moment, its cheerful voice drawing the eyes of the others as it clambered over a low rock ledge. I glanced at my crew, steadying my pony and pulling him back toward the path as the robot waited.

Finally, it tittered at itself, as if amused prematurely by the answer it was about to give, and with a certain air of excitement, it called out, "You put a little boogie in it!" It threw its hands into the air dramatically.

The whole of us burst into laughter, some doubled over on their saddles, others, like Tatiana, with tears streaming down her dark cheeks. It had been too long since we had laughed like that. It was the kind of laughter that you just couldn't recover from, the kind that kept coming up again every time one of us would look at another, and our eyes would meet.

Eventually, it dawned on me that with this robot active, we suddenly had access to information that we never would have been able to figure out otherwise.

"Robot? What year is it?"

I had always wondered that. We had kept track of how many years had passed since the first Oil Day, but we didn't really know what that meant.

The robot's lights blinked into existence.

"The current year is 2276."

Everyone had something to say about that, but unfortunately, I never got the chance to think about it too long. Without warning, my pony leaped sideways beneath me, jarring the reins from my clutch and tossing me unceremoniously to the ground. My shoulder hit first, colliding with the hard prairie and sending me sprawling onto my back with a crack and a wail of pain. It was nothing compared to the scream Buddy let out as he went toppling into the grass in front of me, one leg crumpled beneath him, head thrown back unnaturally over his shoulder.

Other horses spooked, Porter's rearing and nearly sending Tatiana over its back. Wes's mare went galloping away with him over the hill, and the others stomped their hooves, tossing their heads and whinnying warnings.

"Buddy!" I rolled onto my stomach and scrambled to the place where he writhed in pain. I grabbed for his bridle, pulling his head down and trying to steady him, but he kept crying, foam clinging to his bit, his dark eyes wide and full of fear.

"What the hell happened?!"

The others gathered as I started to panic, fingers clutching over his mane and his palomino hide, tugging at the girth of his saddle to give him space to breathe. Porter dropped down and rounded on us, heading for the patch of trees we'd been near when it happened. However, it was the robot that answered my question, approaching brazenly through the crowd as it looked the fallen horse over.

"This animal has been bitten by a highly venomous snake. Due to the small stature and weight of the animal in question, I estimate its chances of survival at less than—"

"That's enough! I don't need no fuckin' estimates. Buddy, he's…he's a good pony! A strong pony! Hell, we made it through a jaguar attack, we made it through *Manhattan*…he's…he's been shot by raiders, tripped down mine shafts, and waded through crocodile-infested rivers to save me. He's strong!" I tried to believe what I was saying, but the more I watched him writhe and pant and the more his leg bled out into the soil that he pawed, the weaker my words became. Eventually they were just a whisper, and I hung my head till I could feel Buddy's warm shoulder against my face.

Porter's hand came to rest on my back, and when she spoke, I could tell she meant it to sound softer than it did.

"Sharkey, you know what you gotta do."

Yeah, I knew. But I wasn't ready. I don't know how I ever was. An hour went by, and the sun crept lower over the horizon, casting a warm golden glow over Buddy's body, and the crimson pool that had welled under his bent leg. I lay there with him, listening to his breath, feeling his chest swell beneath me as my tears soaked through his mane.

"I got Buddy when I was seven years old. He was my first pony. Jack always teased me, sayin' I'd never grow out of him on account I was so scrawny, but when I got tall enough for a horse, I just couldn't bring myself to trade him in. He was a good pony. He was stubborn and pigheaded, chewed on all the barn doors, wouldn't eat nothin' but grain and apples. And he was barn sour half the time. But to me, he was the best pony in the world."

My breath caught in my chest as I rose to my feet, Tatiana stepping forward to wrap her arms around me.

"He knows you love him, Sharkey...and he forgives you. Best friends always do." She reached out to brush away a few tears from my cheek with a finger, and another sob racked through my chest.

I turned away from her, eyes cast briefly toward the others who'd gathered to watch, and then out into the dusk as Buddy panted, wailing out in pain once more.

Slowly, I pulled my pistol from its holster, turning to face my pony, who was struggling weakly, head lifted up to watch me before he laid it back down.

"I...I can't," I said quietly, the finger I had hovering over the trigger shaking. I turned away again, one hand pushed under my hat till it fell to the ground at my back, nails searching through my messy hair. No one spoke, although I am sure they wanted to. There was no other way but this. I knew it. They knew it. Buddy knew it too.

So finally, with a deep, aching breath, I turned toward my companion, looked down into those sweet brown eyes, aimed my pistol between them, and pulled the trigger.

The gunshot made everyone tense, their mounts blowing air through their noses, hooves pawing over the ground beneath them. After a few minutes had passed, my gun still smoking, resting at my side, unholstered and forgotten, Porter stepped up beside me, gesturing down at the body of the pony with her knuckle.

"It's a shame it was venom...waste of a lotta good meat." She meant well. I knew she did. And it was a good point; even dying out here in The Nothing, you could still be useful most times. If you were a dog, you got eaten. If you were a horse, you got eaten. Hell, sometimes the humans got eaten too. At least then your death could save someone.

I closed my eyes and inhaled deep through my nose before I dropped down to a knee to work his tack off. Wasn't any point wasting a saddle and bridle, or a good set of bags either.

"I wish we didn't have to leave him here like this." I breathed, eyes cast down over him. We didn't have but one shovel though, and the others knew how long it would take to dig a big enough hole.

As I rose, the preacher stepped forward, glancing down so his hat tipped over his forehead.

> He's of the colour of the nutmeg.
> And of the heat of the ginger.... he is pure air and fire;
>   and the dull
> elements of earth and water never appear in him, but
> only in patient stillness while his rider mounts
> him; he is indeed a horse, and all other jades you
> may call beasts.

When he finished he gestured toward his own mount, a beautiful old charcoal-colored mare, offering me silently a place on her back. I nodded, taking my seat.

"Robot?"

I asked softly, watching for its listening lights in the dark.

"How far to the nearest town?"

The robot pointed forward, its voice chipper, unperturbed by the scene it had just witnessed.

"The nearest town is Nevada, Missouri. That's eighty-nine miles away from our current location."

I nodded and sighed, looking back over my shoulder for the others who fell in step behind me before I spoke.

"I want everyone to eat, drink, and take a break now if you gotta. It's gonna be a long ride through the night."

Then on we went, one more burden on our shoulders and one less mouth to feed than before.

CHAPTER ELEVEN

PORTER

THEY RODE ON IN THE SHADOWS THE CLOUDS CAST on the prairies, their dark alcoves offering momentary relief from the harsh sun that beat down on their shoulders. Porter couldn't shake the feeling that something important was about to happen. She was just trying to figure out if it was something good or something bad. Either way, she'd rather forget the feeling altogether than have it stalk her through the fields. She always figured it was best not to think about things like that.

Often, she'd dwell on a passage that her father would read her when she was young and the world got scary. He'd say, "All the world's a stage, / And all the men and women merely players. / They have their exits and their entrances, / And one man in his time plays many parts." It helped calm her mind to consider that someone else was writing the story of her life and she was merely acting out her lines. It helped her explain why bad things happened to good people and why sometimes bad people had it the best. It wasn't her fault or their fault either. It was just the way the play was written.

So over the years, she'd come to hate the god whose words her father preached. Because how could he write such a horrible story for them all? Why couldn't they be the ones he favored? Why couldn't it have been Lawrence that was saved, instead of left to rot away in The Nothing with the people she loved?

These are the thoughts that went through Porter's head as she rode, Tatiana's gentle arms around her waist and her eyes on Sharkey's back. She knew her father's old mare couldn't handle two riders for long, but it wouldn't be more than half a day till they reached Nevada. Juliet was a beautiful black mare that her father had had her entire life. She knew the old girl was strong, but even she couldn't last forever.

"You're quiet," Tatiana whispered, her dark curls falling down over Porter's neck as she propped her forehead against her back.

"Yeah." She shrugged gently. "Got a lot on my mind, baby."

Tatiana hummed softly, soft hands winding around so the pads of her thumbs could brush over her wife's wrists.

"Tell me about it," she breathed, chin pressed into her shoulder now.

Porter sighed, clutching the reins of her horse in her fists and tilting her head up, an exasperated expression turned toward the blue sky above them.

"It's more complicated than that...there's a lot of shit we have to think about. I mean no disrespect to our"—She paused, lowering her voice and sitting back in her saddle to slow their red mare to a walk—"I just mean...are you sure you want to do this?"

Tatiana tilted her head, barely able to get a glance at Porter's face under the brim of her hat.

"You mean leave Sharkey?" The accusation in her voice sent a chill down Porter's spine and she clenched her teeth.

"Never."

Tatiana lifted her chin and her arms untangled in defiance.

"No." She clutched the sides of the saddle to keep her balance.

"You don't get to make that decision. We're s'posed to stay together. I mean what are you trying to say, that Sharkey won't make it to the portal? Or that if he did, you'd send him through alone? Or"—she swallowed hard—"or are you sayin' you'd leave me behind and go with him?"

Porter rolled her eyes, kicking her horse back into a trot to join the others who rode ahead of them.

"This is why I didn't want to talk about it."

The path they followed had been carved out of a streambank by deer and zebra. One side rose up, covered in thick grass, compact shrubs, and saplings, until the hill joined the prairie above them, too steep to cut through. The other side dropped off sharply, rich, dark earth full of animal tracks and slides from gators meeting the water below. Every now and then, one of the horses would lose its footing and slide just an inch to the left before catching itself and jerking up toward the forest.

It was a dangerous route the kid had chosen to take them, but Porter understood why he'd made the decision. They were headed straight down the Missouri border, and on one side of them Highway 49 stretched down through Butler, an empty ghost town. Safe city soldiers from Kansas City would use that highway to reach Nevada, a mining town well fortified and protected by the United Alliance.

Nevada wasn't somewhere they wanted to spend very much time, but Porter knew they'd be able to restock on supplies and find Sharkey a new horse. She winced, glancing down from the spot she'd been staring into Sharkey's head and over the ginger neck of her mare. She often forgot how young Sharkey really was.

"Hey, kid," she called, sidling up to her father's horse as the path widened and diverted away from the stream bank. A monkey screeched and leapt through the branches above them.

Sharkey glanced back. He'd been quiet for hours, but he grunted something of a reply.

Porter went on. "I am sorry about your day. It's been shit, huh?"

Sharkey made a noise, half a laugh through his nose. "Yeah, well, there'll be better ones, right?"

Porter looked away, toward the tree line they rode toward. "I don't know." She leaned forward as the horses jogged up the incline. She felt Tatiana behind her mirroring the movement, and as she awaited Sharkey's response, her wife's arms finally wound back around her waist, a welcome comfort.

Sharkey watched her as Juliet sidestepped and settled in the clearing they'd rode into, the stream far behind them now, no longer visible beneath the underbrush and the trees they'd come out of. Wes trotted ahead, arms spread out to either side, reins abandoned around his saddle horn as he let out a whoop. His dark bay, Shorty, seemed to share in his celebration, tossing her shaggy mane and prancing into the clearing like a yearling filly. Porter and Sharkey exchanged a humored glance, and as they both pulled their horses around to follow Wes into the field, Sharkey finally replied.

"Well, hell, if there ain't no better days than this one, what the hell's the point of all this?"

Porter looked as if she was about to answer, but the robot shoved itself unceremoniously through the woods behind them, tumbling out into the path and exclaiming in that eerily cheerful voice, "Good news, everyone! We are only two miles away from Nevada, Missouri!"

Something like dread passed over Sharkey's face, but Porter had a hard time reading his expression as he turned away from her. The group rode on, the shape of the tall, gated fence that stretched around the perimeter of the town on the horizon growing ever larger.

It didn't really dawn on Porter what she'd said before until the gates of the city were close enough that two snipers could be seen in their towers on either side of it. The sight was unrelated, but it brought her enough clarity that she jogged to Sharkey's side in a hurry, one hand reaching across the divide between them to clutch his nearest arm.

"Hey, kid," she barked. "I'm sorry about Buddy and what I said about eatin' him. I shouldn't've said that."

Sharkey opened his mouth, but it's the robot's voice that spoke instead, bringing the group to a sudden standstill.

"Warning! My internal sensors have detected I am within 500 feet of a U.A. Wi-Fi tower or central net hub. If you will excuse me, my programming dictates I must report for routine maintenance and updates!"

The robot started forward, a pep in its mechanical march that continued even after Sharkey leaped from the preacher's saddle to tackle it.

"*Whoa*! What the fuck are you talkin' about?! You can't go in there! Porter, Wes, grab that rope—"

Several bodies lunged forward to intervene. Sharkey was on the ground with the robot in a chokehold, Porter had the rope wrapped halfway around its torso and one of its silver arms, and Wes had the thing's legs.

The trio grappled with the robot haphazardly—its artificial strength more than they were prepared to counter—but eventually they were able to drag it back into the woods behind them.

"All right..." Sharkey ran a hand through his hair before he tucked his hat back over his head.

"Wes, Preacher, you two sit tight here and make sure this thing don't move an inch. We'll be back before long. Go ahead and set up camp, and I will get us some dinner while we're in there. Oh, I'm gonna take your horse, Wes. Got some things to haul..." Sharkey trailed off as he grabbed his pony's saddle from the ground and worked it onto the back of Wes's mount. He gave the horse a gentle pat before loading up the rest of the scrap they had.

Wes side-eyed Sharkey and waggled a finger at him. "Hey, you be nice to Shorty now. She neck reins all right, and her mouth's real sensitive, so don't go yanking her bit around."

He went on for a bit, but Sharkey gave him a look.

"I'll treat 'er like a princess, okay?" His hands were gentle when they took her reins.

The three set off once more for the towering gates on the horizon, this time more prepared, though it was still a nerve-racking experience. First the snipers got them in their scopes, and the hairs on the back of Porter's neck stood on end. It was a strange sensation, knowing that at any second, if a stranger decided...you'd be dead. You could know they had no reason to, but it wouldn't make a difference.

Then the guards, two of them, both with their shiny uniforms on and their assault rifles clutched in their hands, turned toward them expectantly.

"Business?" one barked, holding a gloved hand out to stop them. The other readied the lever that would let them through, but he didn't dare pull it yet.

Sharkey put on his best smile, one hand reaching up to swipe his hat from his head so he could use it to gesture toward Nevada.

"Oh, we're just passin' through, sir. Won't be any trouble."

The guard snorted, not quite believing Sharkey's claim but allowing it for the time.

"Yeah, I reckon you won't be. And if you are,"—he grabbed him by the shirt and dragged him up to his face—"I'll find you, and I'll string your skinny ass up over this gate as a warning. You understand me, boy?"

Sharkey clenched his jaw, one hand outstretched toward Porter, who had immediately squared her shoulders, ready to attack.

"Yes, sir."

Porter let out the breath she'd been holding. It's the next words out of the man's mouth that had all three of them groaning.

"Guns ain't allowed. You can pick them up on your way out of town."

They stepped through the gates and into the bustling street, unarmed, surrounded by safe city soldiers, and all equally certain this was one of the stupidest things they'd done yet.

"I want to get the fuck out of here," Porter muttered, working a joint out of her pocket and into her lips. She was shaking her head even as Tatiana moved on into the street. From where they stood, they could look all the way down the center of town, one wide, paved road littered with people, shops, food stalls, barking dogs, and horses. Porter had never seen anything like it in her life. It was nothing like the dreary streets of Lawrence, where maybe you'd see a few familiar faces on your way to the bar. No, this was a real, proper town, where the shops had more things for sale than she'd ever seen in her life.

"This place is amazing!" Tatiana burst forward with open arms, but Porter was able to snag her by an elbow before she got too far.

"Whoa, there. Before you go all crazy on me, we are all meeting back at the gates in two hours."

Tatiana nodded, grinning, eyes everywhere but on Porter's face. Porter turned away, content to let Tatiana loose, but her wife's voice ebbed through the noise.

"Babe?"

Porter turned toward her, a question in her eyes.

"Would you ever..." Tatiana trailed off, grabbing for Porter's hands. Sharkey pretended he wasn't listening, but Porter knew he was.

"Would you ever consider...staying in a place like this?"

Porter opened her mouth to reply, but Sharkey interrupted, one hand clasped on Porter's shoulder. She wasn't entirely sure why he'd done it.

"Come on, let's get going."

Tatiana turned and headed straight for a clothing shop. She bypassed a huge, gaudy crimson dress in the window and beelined for a baby blue skirt set on the far wall, much to Porter's dismay.

"Hey, we got a budget, you hear?" she called back, but Tatiana was already gone, vanished into the crowd.

"Well, we're not gonna see her for the rest of the day." Porter clapped a hand over Sharkey's shoulder and moved him forward into the crowd, casting one last worried glance back over her shoulder to watch the shape of her wife disappear.

They walked on, heads down strategically when soldiers passed by. Something about the density of people in the dusty streets made Porter feel lonelier than any night she'd spent under the stars with only her horse for company.

After a few blocks, Sharkey cleared his throat.

"You know, you've been loyal to me for a real long time, Porter. If...I just mean, you know...if you wanted to stay, I'd forgive you. Eventually."

Porter set her jaw for a moment, eyes busy in the crowd, like she wasn't paying him any attention. She replied, though, and her voice was full of some kind of promise she'd never used before.

"You kiddin' me? And miss the look on yer face when you see that portal? Not a chance."

Their eyes met for a moment as the sun shone and set the cloud of dust on fire around them.

Finding the stable was easy after that, though the second they'd set their sights on it, just the eave of the barn visible between shops, the stable doors clattered open and a beautiful white mare tore out into the street. She had half a halter over her nose and a lead rope dragging behind her, and before the fat stable keeper could snatch her up, she leaped clear over a wagon passing through the intersection by the barn and took off into the parting crowd.

"Somebody grab that fuckin' horse!" the stable keeper called, and before Porter could intervene, Sharkey had thrown the reins of Wes's mount at her and taken off on foot. Porter cursed, casting the end of her blunt down into the dirt before heading after him.

"Careful, Sharkey!" Porter hollered, but she knew it wouldn't do much good. He'd already cornered the mare, got a rope around her neck, and swung up onto her bareback. She bucked a few times, but she wasn't the first horse who'd tried to throw the kid. Even so, Porter was tense, prepared to rush forward to try to drag him out from underneath her hooves.

Before long, she settled, and once she did, Sharkey slipped down beside her, one hand smoothing over the pale hair between her wild eyes.

"Well, if anyone could tame a sour horse, it'd be you. Whatcha thinkin'?"

Sharkey combed fingers through her snowy mane and flashed

a grin, watching Porter for a moment as he led the mare back toward the barn she'd come from. They'd both seen the whip marks on her flanks right away, and all it took was a look exchanged between them for Porter to know Sharkey was taking that horse with him.

"Thanks, lad. Fucking animal's crazy. Gonna sell her for meat and save myself some trouble. What can I do for you today?" The stable keeper spat through his bushy mustache, one hand slapping over his round stomach while the other grabbed for the mare's reins. Sharkey moved them from his reach with one hand.

"I'm gonna take this horse here. Saddle and bridle for her too." Sharkey said, nodding firmly like it wasn't really debatable. Porter watched wearily, shoulders squared, eyes steely as the stable keeper laughed.

"The butcher'll pay me a few ingots for her. What do you have that's better than that?"

Sharkey motioned for Porter to bring Wes's horse forward, and when she did, he hauled the little saddle from her back.

"Couple ingots and a child's saddle. Can't find these anywhere. Made it myself." Sharkey turned the saddle over in his arms, nodding toward the underside where his and his father's initials could be seen burnt into the leather. Porter knew damn well that had been the only thing Sharkey and his father had ever worked on together, and as Sharkey handed it over, she lowered her head to hide the pain in her eyes.

"Pfftt." The stable keeper looked less than impressed, but he shrugged his shoulders. "I guess it'll do. Get her outta my sight."

The mare left with Sharkey that evening, and if Porter hadn't already known what he'd say, she would have told him how noble he looked riding her down the street. The lights showed through her snowy mane, and her pale blue eyes looked silver as she tossed her head. The sight was almost intimidating, the way the dust rose behind her, Sharkey's head down, one hand pushing his hat up over his hair. On that horse, he finally looked like a man.

"Now don't get all fucking sappy on me." He grinned at her from the other side of the street once he'd caught her staring.

They'd stopped in front of a bar, and as Sharkey dismounted, Porter shook her head, snorting through flared nostrils. "Ha! I don't care how fancy your horse is; you still look like a skinny little brat to me."

They grinned at each other as they stepped into the bar, this one nothing like the Free Place. It was all lit up with different-colored lanterns strung across the ceiling so that all the bulbs reflected in the wall of glass bottles behind the counter. Every stool matched the upholstery on the bench seats along the walls, and the floor was made of dark polished wood. There was something comforting about its atmosphere, and every face that turned to watch them as they entered looked content somehow.

It was a strange feeling, realizing that this town was just like Lawrence, and that there was no difference in the prostitutes who peered over the balcony upstairs or the little girl no older than Chesser who pushed her head between two long skirts to see. Porter couldn't bear to meet her eyes, and Sharkey swallowed hard beside her, moving on toward the bar, where things weren't quite as complicated.

"Double whiskey. Cheap stuff. Porter?"

"Same."

Sharkey nodded, glancing back over the display behind the bartender. He pointed to a handle of dark liquor, adding it to the tab.

Porter had her back to the counter, surveying the room like she always did when her boss was occupied. Out of the corner of her eye, Porter watched a weaselly man peel quietly out of the crowd. Sharkey saw him too, but didn't seem to register him as a threat quite yet, content in the knowledge that if anyone could take care of the both of them, it was Porter. The man's greasy black hair clung to his head like a cap, and the product in it stuck to the sides of his face. Even his mustache was waxed, and it curled around his sunken cheeks like black paint. Porter had never seen a man who looked so much like a rat—and the second he propped himself up against the counter beside her, she knew he would be trouble.

"Hey there, how ya doin'?" he sang, one hand raising his beer while his eyebrows danced up into his hairline. Almost immediately, before Porter could even raise her fist to punch him out, he had slumped down over the countertop in obvious dismay.

"I'm sorry," he said softly, staring down into the last of his beer that he clutched between spindly fingers. Sharkey smirked, watching for Porter's reaction. She rolled her eyes, lowering her fist and snatching her shot off the counter.

"Whaddaya want?" She knocked her shot back and slammed the glass down hard enough to snap the man's eyes up.

He winced, picking at the loose string of his fingerless gloves.

"Well, if I'm bein' honest with myself, I just want to get the hell outta this fuckin' town. Goddamn soldiers everywhere breathin' down your neck. It ain't right, and it's cursed, I tell ya. Won't let ya walk in, won't let ya leave." He went to sit, but fumbled over the edge of the stool, trying and failing to scoot it under him several times before he was seated on it properly.

"What's any of that got to do with us?"

Sharkey eyed her, but he'd busied himself talking shop with the barkeeper and he trusted her to handle the situation.

With desperation in his voice as he lit up a smoke in shaking fingers, he said, "My name's Lionel, by the way. And I can do things. Tons of things, I am great at things. And, uh, I got connections in towns all across the country. I can fix things."

Porter went to stand and step away from him but he grabbed her arm. Porter reached for her dagger.

"Porter. *Porter.*" Sharkey peered over from his stool, expression firm. "What the hell are you doing?" He was ready to step in, but he didn't yet, eyes on the door where armed guards could appear at any moment.

Porter smirked, shoving the man back against the bar as she sheathed her knife.

"Makin' friends?" Sharkey turned his back to grab the handle of whiskey he'd ordered. Porter gave him a look and shrugged.

She fixed Lionel with those steely eyes, brow set, one finger pointed out toward him. "So you can do stuff? Big deal." She worked a joint between her lips, puffing on it for a moment. "We're tryin' to get to Dallas. Ya got any of those connections between here and there?"

Lionel lit up, curiosity in his dark eyes. "Oh sure! There's this great family in Tulsa, about a week from here. Heading that same direction. They can get you guys anything you need for a big trip like that."

Porter seemed to be contemplating things, and although Sharkey had been listening the entire time, he pretended like he wasn't. She cast her eyes down for a moment, huffing softly into her empty glass.

"If I let ya come, ya promise me you won't fuck over my crew."

Lionel looked around like she must have been talking to someone else.

"Oh, shit. You...you're serious? You'd actually let me tag along?"

"If," Porter countered, jabbing that finger into Lionel's chest, "you can be useful. Got it? If we get to Tulsa and find out you've been lyin' to us, we'll string you up by your feet an' leave ya for the lions. Got it?"

"Yes, ma'am."

Sharkey peered over at them again, brows rising.

"You two good? Let's go, Porter."

Porter elbowed Lionel in the ribs, nodding toward Sharkey absently.

"Lionel here's comin' with. Ya got a problem with that, boss?"

Sharkey smirked, making a face under the shadow of his hat.

"Nope. So long as we can get the fuck out of here."

They left together, horses led behind them, gentle banter ebbing out into the dusk that fell over the town of Nevada. And once they'd left—Tatiana holding up the things she'd bought and walking backward—and those gates were far behind them, something like peace settled over Porter's restless soul.

CHAPTER TWELVE

THE COFFEE HOUSE

RICKY WATCHED FROM THE HILLSIDE AS SHARKEY raced that little pony as fast as he could down the straightaway between the Kansas City feedlots. He watched as the others followed him, and from his vantage on the hill, he could see the piles of carcasses by the walls long before the stench of death found him. It didn't take a genius to put the bodies together with the closed gate and the way the group took off in a somber gallop into the prairies a few minutes later to tell him Sharkey's plans had changed.

"Well, I'll be damned. He actually got that thing runnin'?" Kent asked from behind him, moving up onto the peak beside him and peering over the edge as they watched the tiny shape of the robot clamber away in the distance.

"I don't give a shit about the robot," Ricky said, tracking the group as they moved.

"I just want to know where the hell they're goin' now. Not back to Lawrence. What d'ya reckon, Kent? Reckon we should follow him?"

Kent fixed him with a curious look, one brow lifting.

"Well, hell, Ricky, you're the boss here, not me. You did promise Mama, though. Said you'd keep him safe till he got wherever he's goin', and, well,"—he glanced back out over the prairies, the group barely visible over the hill now—"he's still goin' somewhere, ain't he?"

Ricky made a noise, looking back over his shoulder at the others. He watched Clay playing with a flower he'd found, big hands mangling the petals. He watched Jon, looking over the larger man with his arms folded and his head shaking, an ever-patient smile on his face. He watched Mayra, with the reins of the horses in her hands and her fierce gaze on him, awaiting an

99

order. Then he looked to Crystal, and when their eyes met, the most beautiful smile spread across her lips.

"Whatever you decide, Ricky, we'll follow you."

Her voice didn't seem to bring Ricky as much relief as perhaps she'd meant it. And instead, he lowered his head, one hand rubbing over his arm.

"If we do this, it's gonna be dangerous. The Nothin' always is. And I don't know where we're even going, or how long we'll be gone. Ya'll can go home right now if ya want. And don't give me that 'we are family' bullshit. I know it, and I'd still rather you go."

He waited for a moment, looking at them all, and no one moved. So, with a firm nod and a last look over the distant walls of the safe city behind them, they mounted and started off once more over the rolling Kansas hills.

■

The weather was pleasant enough that a gentle breeze turned up their collars and tossed their hats from their heads as they rode, though the sun peeked through the clouds after a while and warmed their saddles and the backs of their mounts. They'd lost sight of Sharkey hours earlier, but they had a good view of their tracks on the prairie.

Kent came up on Ricky's right, close enough that their horses bickered at each other with their lips pulled back. Ricky tugged his horse's face away, one elbow jutting out to press into Kent's side playfully. Their knees brushed in their stirrups, and once they'd settled into a comfortable pace, Kent gestured forward with a tip of his head.

"You all right with this whole riding into the unknown? I mean who the fuck knows where that kid's going. You know he cooks up all kinds of stupid plans in his head, and with that robot..." Kent trailed off, shrugging his shoulders.

Ricky watched him, unfamiliar with the uncertainty in his friend's eyes. What had changed between the peak of the hill and the trail they rode now. Was it fear? He had never seen fear in him before, not even during wartime, not plagues, not throngs of enemies, not even death.

He pulled his horse around to halt him, both animals throwing their heads up in protest, but it needed to be said, and he had to look him in the eye to say it properly.

"You listen here, Kent. I've been savin' your sorry ass since we were kids. I ain't stopping now, ya hear me?"

Kent nodded, a hint of a smile playing over his scruffy face. Ricky knew the other man well enough to know that it meant he understood, but just for good measure, he reached across the neck of Kent's horse to shove his head away, a grin on his face.

Just then, as Ricky was turning his horse back toward the trail they had been heading down, Crystal, who had gone on ahead, let out a shrill scream. The boys raced to her, hats in their hands, startled eyes on Crystal and Mayra and whatever lay before them that had caused them such a fright.

"Is that...?" Kent started to ask, but Ricky already knew the answer.

"Buddy."

Ricky looked over the carcass of the slain pony with a deep frown and his hands clenched into fists over his reins. He dismounted and knelt beside him, one hand moving slowly over Buddy's white mane until it met his shoulder blades, where he patted gently over his withers.

"What do you reckon happened? Hell, Sharkey loved that damn pony! Look at that!" Kent gestured to the bullet hole between his eyes.

Crystal couldn't bear to look at the sight for long, and she'd moved off with her paint mare in tow, soothing the horse gently whether she had been bothered or not.

Ricky took a deep breath, hand moving down over Buddy's leg, where dark bruises and swollen skin gave away the real cause of his death.

"Snake got him. I reckon Sharkey knew he wasn't gonna make it. Put him out of his misery. Better end for his damn horse than Peggie.

"Get the shovels, everyone. Looks like we got one more grave to dig."

■

It was harder digging a grave for a horse than for a human. Had to be bigger—and getting the body in was the hardest part of all. They managed it, but by the time they got him buried, the sun was well down, and the trail they'd been following had been taken by the night.

"You know I got that pony for him?" Ricky said over the crackling fire, shoulders hunched, arms resting over his knees as he watched Kent across from him.

"I remember," he replied, glancing down into the flames before he grinned.

"Papa Shark sent you off for a man's horse from market. An'...an you said—"

"—He'll get a man's horse when he's a man."

Kent shook his head, working the lid off his flask.

"He was, what, seven? You came back with that scrawny fucking colt. I'll never forget the look on Jack's face. But Sharkey? I've never seen him happier."

Ricky swallowed, nodding along to Kent's words and taking the flask when it was passed his way. He glanced at the others as they strapped up tent poles and tarps, Crystal fumbling with hers while Clay and Jon argued over something by the trees where the horses were tied.

"What's goin' on in there?" Kent asked softly, using the bit of kindling he'd grabbed from the pile to gesture toward Ricky's head. He shoved it away, swiping his hat from his head and turning it over in his hands. With his hair down over his ears, he looked younger than he was. Maybe it was the orange glow of the fire between them that hid the lines in his skin.

"I think I'm gonna make a cup o' coffee. You want one?"

Kent sighed, nodding as he sat back in his folding chair, head tilted up over the back so he could see the stars through the jungle canopy above them. He wondered absently if there had always been so many up there.

Ricky worked carefully, rough hands gentle when they held his mug and the screen top he'd fixed over it, slow even when he measured out the grounds and the last of the condensed cream from his saddlebag. After he handed Kent his cup, he looked back at his own, cradled there between his dirt-covered palms, the steam rolling over his skin, curling around the nicks and cuts and the divots in his nails.

"Ya gonna drink that?" Kent asked, looking briefly between the cup of coffee and Ricky's blue eyes. He was thinking about it, turning the cup this way and then another.

"Maybe." He shrugged his shoulders and nodded toward the cup in Kent's hand. "How's yours?"

Kent smiled, raising his mug.

"Perfect."

Ricky didn't reply, but he laughed through his nose, head down for a moment before he sat up to watch Kent drink for a while. Eventually he took a sip of his own, but he didn't seem to have anything at all to say about it.

Hours passed like that, when Clay came and Ricky asked him to read the stars to tell them where they were. Eventually, the others went to sleep, and Crystal pressed gentle kisses on both of their heads before going too. Only Kent and Ricky remained, their backs in their folding chairs and their hands on their knees. When the silence had grown long and peaceful and only the buzz of insects and the calls of primates broke the still, Kent spoke again.

"You know I always wondered, Ricky, is it the milk that makes it bad? The sugar? The beans? What makes it perfect?" When she heard her name, Ricky's dog lifted her tawny head from the ground at his feet, tail wagging behind her.

Ricky stayed quiet a moment, glancing down over Bean and

the forgotten cup of coffee, half full and cold, beside her. After a while, he sucked in another breath, chest heaving as he worked his hat back over his head.

"I may never know. Sometimes I feel like such an idiot for even giving a damn. Seems like there's more important shit to worry about, right?"

"Nah, you kiddin' me? What? Scrappin' and shittin', and eatin', and dyin'? What's more important?" Kent looked away, combing his fingers through his hair.

"The way I see it, Ricky, in this fucked up world, ya gotta find somethin' or someone that makes it all mean somethin'. And whether that's a cup of coffee, or a girl, or a man, or a book, or a fuckin' portal...don't make no difference, so long as it means somethin' to ya."

Ricky watched him, eyes soft and lidded, arms back over his knees as he peered forward through the soft glow of the dying embers in the firepit. And when he spoke, his voice was quiet, kept between the two of them by a soft breeze that carried the smoke up through the trees.

"Well," he said, pushing himself up to his feet and reaching across to snag Kent's hat off his head, "You're a hell of a lot smarter than you look." His words were teasing, and he tossed the hat back over Kent's knee before he turned away toward his tent. Kent called back to him though, and what he said stopped him in his tracks. He didn't look back, but he stared out into the dark jungle for a long time afterward.

"Remember, I'm gonna be there when you find that perfect cup of coffee."

■

Picking up Sharkey's trail was easy enough the next day: three sets of horse tracks and the strange, flat footprints the robot left deep in the ground. It didn't take them long to find the town they led to or the tall, guarded gates and the noise of crowds behind them. Ricky looked skeptical, and before they even thought about going in, he took the time to hide his gun in one of his tall leather boots.

"All right, everyone. I don't like the look of this place, but Sharkey probably came through here lookin' for another horse. If he found one, I reckon he's already heading out of town, so keep your eye out for his people. And remember, we got a time limit here. I don't want to stay in there for long."

Crystal couldn't hide the excitement on her face as she edged up to Ricky's side, delicate hands clasped eagerly behind her.

"Are we all goin' in, Ricky?"

"Yes, Crystal. We're all goin' in. Come on." He side-eyed Kent, watching the other man as he tucked his own weapon away and out of sight under his shirt. This wasn't the first time the two of them had been in a situation like this, and they both knew better than to walk up with full holsters.

Sure enough, their weapons were the first things the guards attempted to confiscate on their approach, and both Ricky and Kent had their hands up in the air before the guards even asked.

"No weapons here, sir," they chanted together, turning around when asked, all well behaved. In fact everything went smoothly enough until one of the guards decided to pat Crystal down "just in case."

"Touch her and you'll lose that hand," Ricky snapped, snatching the gloved hand that reached for her waist and shoving it away. The other guard interceded, grabbing his buddy by his arm and dragging him backward toward their post. Unfortunately it only got worse from there.

"Well, you better get that mutt of yours on a leash," the guard said, pointing one of his gloved fingers down at Bean, who, as always, sat obediently at her master's feet. She tilted her head, looking up toward Ricky for any signal that she'd done something wrong. Ricky scowled.

"What did you just call my dog?"

The guard brought his assault rifle up from his side, and

before the situation could get worse, Kent slipped his belt from his pants and looped it over Bean's neck.

"Everything's good here, officer," Kent said.

"It ain't worth it, George, just forget it." The same guard, who still held the other back, spoke. "Go on!" Half his attention was still on the man he had pinned back against the gate. Kent was just as prepared to pull Ricky away, and one of his hands still hovered on Ricky's shoulder before they all turned and made for the bustling streets. It was an unbelievable sight for most of the party, and Ricky knew as much by the excited gasps he heard behind him.

First, Clay went charging off toward a shop down the way. Some manner of tools for looking at stars in the window that Ricky wasn't familiar with. Jon rushed after him hollering something. Ricky wanted anything for Clay that might help him settle his mind though, and he knew his one talent in life was knowing exactly where they were by the stars. Not even Jon knew how he did it. Then Mayra and Crystal had vanished into a clothing shop to their left, and Ricky and Kent stood alone once more in a bustling crossroads.

"I hate crowds," Kent said, turning his collar up as strangers brushed by them. Ricky was all too familiar with his friend's distaste for pretty much any company but his own and gave him a soft look before heading off down the street. Luckily for both of them, Ricky's presence alone seemed to be enough to divide the crowd. Ricky walked like he owned any path he followed, and if someone or something got in his way? Well the obstacle wouldn't be there for long.

After a few minutes wandering the streets, a commotion down the way drew their attention. Both men pressed their backs to the wall of the nearest building to watch Sharkey and that white mare in the alleyway across the street. They exchanged a look and headed back to find the others.

The sun was going down by the time they saw it, that old neon sign flickering along a line of shops on their right.

"Is that...?" Kent had barely begun to ask when Ricky damn near sprinted toward it. He stood there in the street for a long time, bathed in the yellow light of the sign that read COFFEE HOUSE, OPEN 24/7.

"Ya gonna go in?" Kent asked, stepping up to Ricky's side and nudging him gently with his elbow. Ricky looked perplexed, like he wasn't really sure if what he was seeing was real or not.

"Gimme a second." He held a hand out, blue eyes still lost, staring like he was looking at some otherworldly being or the first sunset he'd ever seen. Then very slowly, and with a certain level of grace in his steps he didn't often show, he opened the door and stepped into the building.

"Um, sir, no dogs allowed," the barista began, one of her dark hands still clenched over the handle of some fancy machine she was using. Ricky didn't seem to hear her. Or, Kent decided, pretended not to. He was too busy looking every which way at once, up into the shelves of coffee cups on the walls, over the tables with their little vases of flowers, and the counter, where several other perplexed workers stood watching him. The woman raised her voice, hands propped over her wide hips now.

"I *said* no dogs allowed. Can't you read?"

Kent lowered his head, muttering under his breath, "Actually..."

But Ricky interrupted him, a frown on his face as he started forward to the counter.

"Make me a coffee," he ordered, much to the surprise of all those who attended the little shop. The women scowled, but one turned away to start another machine up in preparation for his order.

"Fine," the barista snapped, rolling her eyes as she turned away to get his drink.

Ricky took a seat while Kent tried his best to smooth things over, staying behind at the counter's edge while they worked.

"He really is a nice guy, I swear. I mean not as nice as me but—"

Ricky cleared his throat and Kent flashed the woman a wink before he plopped down across from his boss at one of the little tables. He eyed the vase and the flower for a moment before another shit-eating grin flashed across his face.

"Wow, Ricky, I had no idea you felt this way about me, taking me on a date in the city." He ducked before Ricky could swipe his hat over his face, but he saw the hint of that smile playing over Ricky's lips.

Suddenly, Kent got to his feet and darted toward something on the wall behind them, eyes the size of saucers.

"Holy fuck! Ricky, look at this, a real French press! Can you believe it? I didn't know any of these were left!"

Ricky stood, shouldering past him to get a better look. It was a beautiful thing, all made of glass and stainless steel. It may have been the most beautiful thing Ricky had ever seen in his life. And while Ricky stared at it, Kent watched him.

"How much?" He called, pointing, but the woman behind the counter scoffed.

"Not for sale," she said. Kent's face dropped, shoulders slumped down, as he turned back. Ricky had already stepped away though, and he sat in that chair again with his back to him.

"Forget it, Kent, I don't need no fancy piece of doo-dad. Never have, never will."

But Kent couldn't let it go, and he slammed his hands over the table as he came to face him again.

"But what if that's what makes it perfect, Ricky? How can you just sit there? Hell, this might be the last one."

But Ricky was already shaking his head.

"I said forget it, Kent."

Kent's voice was quiet when he replied, and he looked away, eyes cast down toward the ground beneath them.

"All right."

Just then, the barista from before set Ricky's drink down in front of him, and before Kent could even think to react, all hell broke loose.

"What the fuck is this?!" Ricky shouted, staring down at the glass of iced coffee in front of him, condensation trickling down and collecting by his hand that laid across the table. Had Kent known, had he any inclination as to what kind of coffee they served at this coffee house, he would have turned Ricky away at the door. He would have never let him in. In one swift movement, Ricky got to his feet so quickly that the table between them overturned, spilling the water from the vase and the coffee across the floor. The vase shattered, glass washing over their boots.

"*Ricky*!" Kent yelled, but it was too late. Ricky'd already lost his temper, and he had the gun from his boot pulled and pointed at the machine behind the counter. One of the women screamed, and before Kent could reach him, a single shot rang out through the room. Steam burst from the split metal, hissing, and sent the other woman leaping for cover behind the counter. Ricky stuffed his gun away and turned on the heel of his boot, snagged Kent by the scruff of his collar, and pushed him out into the street.

"Get up!" he said, and already soldiers shouted in the distance, collecting at an intersection a few blocks down and pointing toward the source of the commotion. Both men were saddled and tearing off down the street quicker than any of those soldiers could stuff their whistles into their mouths, though, and even Bean kept pace, running as fast as she could through the parting crowd behind them.

It didn't take long for both horses to break out into the stretch of field on the outskirts of town, well past the other set of gates opposite the ones they'd come through. Ricky's gelding reared when he whooped, and Kent rounded on him, his laughter already ringing out into the night that had fallen around them. Ricky leaned over his saddle, and Kent was trying to catch his breath.

"You're one crazy son of a bitch. You know that, Ricky? Ain't no other man in the world I'd rather ride with." He was grinning wider than maybe he ever had, and Ricky clapped a hand over his shoulder as they walked out into the dark together, as always, side by side.

"You know," Ricky went on, giving him a look, "You're *really* bad at keeping me outta trouble."

By the time they found the camp, they'd been riding around the edges of town for hours, and Crystal had already roasted a boar over the fire.

"I knew you two would make it home eventually. How much trouble did you manage to get into?" She grinned over the flames as she tentatively stripped some meat from the portion balanced over her knees. Mayra grunted, mirroring her smile as she looked up to greet them.

"Oh, you know us. Ricky here made some friends. I ended up dancin' in the middle of town because public displays are *my* favorite thing. Oh, and we saw Sharkey and Porter." Kent waved a hand about casually as he told the story, and Ricky, from his place behind him where he worked at untacking the horses, smiled to himself as he listened to the group laugh together.

He only noticed Crystal's hair once she'd tossed it dramatically over her shoulder about a hundred times and finally fixed her long braids with an inquisitive look.

"You turned your hair pink."

Crystal squealed loudly enough that he looked around for the wild animal that had caused it.

"Don't you just love it, Ricky?"

"I love it," Kent interjected, grinning as he reached across to tug at one of her braided pigtails playfully. She shoved his hand away, wrinkling her nose at him and sticking her tongue out. Just then Mayra returned, though Ricky hadn't noticed she'd left. Kent's jaw dropped, and he pointed.

"Holy shit! I never thought I'd see you in a dress, Mayra!" He whooped as he pushed himself to his feet to get a better look at her. She'd bought the crimson gown in the front window, and Ricky looked it over with a smile.

"You look beautiful, Mayra," he said, nodding his head firmly as a huge smile split the woman's usually stern face. She did a spin, and as the night wore on, Jon and Clay joined them, Clay busy with the sextant Jon had bought him in Nevada.

"Where we at, Clay?" Ricky asked, glancing up into the sky.

"Well, well that's Orion's belt, sir. That means we are 123 miles southeast from Lawrence."

Ricky watched over them all, one arm resting over his bent knee, the other down at his side so his fingers could curl gently through Bean's fur. Eventually, as the fire turned to embers, the others made their way into their tents one by one, until Ricky and Kent sat, as they had so many times before, facing one another with only the faint glow of crackling, burning wood between them.

"Hey...I know you've never let me before, but...tomorrow... can I make your coffee for you?" Kent's voice was quiet when he spoke, and when Ricky looked up toward his eyes, there was something turning in them, something that made him consider his reply.

"All right, but just this once," Ricky said, expression still weary.

Kent rose, saluted mockingly, and went to his tent, leaving Ricky to watch as even Bean trotted away after him. Sometimes he wondered whose dog Bean really was. Ricky shook his head, chuckling softly under his breath, as he kicked what was left of the crumbling log into the middle of the ash pile, and with something like contentment in his heart, he left to find his bed.

CHAPTER THIRTEEN

IN THE NIGHT

SEVEN GUNSHOTS WOKE ME FROM MY SLEEP THAT night, stirring the horses—and the birds from their roosts in the grass. I grabbed for my weapon and rolled out of my tent quickly, eyes searching through the shadows, following the commotion to the dim lights of the city beneath us, at the bottom of the hill.

From my vantage point, I could look all the way down into the streets of Nevada, over the tall guarding walls, and I could just barely see soldiers gathering. Whatever had happened, it wasn't anything I wanted my people involved with.

"Come on guys, pack it up. I don't know, but it ain't worth lookin' into." The others didn't need to be roused from their tents. Porter stepped out first, shouldering her jacket on and nodding toward the city lights.

"That was a lotta shots. What do you reckon?"

I shook my head, tossing my horse's saddle over her back and working the bit into her mouth.

"Fuck if I know, but we ain't sticking around to find out. Make sure everyone's ready. Tell 'em we're headin' for Tulsa."

Only the robot seemed to do what I told it to. Eventually, however, we all managed to mount up. And although even the horses seemed reluctant to ride out into the night, they did their best, walking slowly with their heads still heavy from sleep and their ears alert to the dangerous noises that sounded around us.

"You know, in Nevada, it's customary for folks to have a cup of coffee when they wake up and, you know, for the sun to be out," Lionel whined from his scraggly mount, throwing one of his hands up into the air to make his point clear. The robot tittered something behind us, its inlaid lights casting shadows of our group up over the trunks of trees that we passed by.

Eventually, the sun began to climb up from between the hills, golden arms reaching into the dark sky.

Porter and I rode together, Tatiana asleep against the preacher's back ahead of us.

"You figure out what yer gonna name her yet?"

I glance down over the pale neck of the mare I rode, reaching down to pat her shoulder a few times.

"I dunno. I was thinkin' Dallas, since she's gonna be the one to take me there, ya know?"

Porter grinned, nodding. "That's a good name. King Lear and I agree, don't we, boy?" She clapped her hand on her gelding's neck, rubbing a few circles over his red hair. It was strange, riding a full-sized horse for the first time, sitting in a full-sized saddle. I slipped more than I used to, and it forced me to hold on with my legs a little more when the trail got rough.

Through a group of saplings ahead of us, something caught my eye that had me halting the group rather suddenly.

"See somethin', boss?" Porter asked, stepping up beside me and glancing ahead. I pointed toward the shape of a wagon sitting out on a dirt road ahead of us. We dismounted quietly and led our horses out into the road.

"Be on alert. Might not be abandoned."

We moved closer, where the wagon sat on three wheels. The fourth lay on its side in a rut beside it. Just then a rifle cocks, and before I could react, a man lunged out from the wagon's interior.

"Get away from us!" He had the muzzle of a rifle level with my head. Porter and Wes were faster than the old man though, and they both had their pistols on him.

"Reckon you're not in the position to be making those kinda demands," Porter said. He lowered his weapon and stepped back toward the wagon.

"What happened here?" I asked as several faces peered out from behind the curtains that lay across the wagon's back. There were children, two at least, and a woman with a kind, almond-shaped face. She watched me through dark eyes, her long black hair strewn over soft brown cheeks. The robot had stepped up beside me, and the children cowered from it.

The man who guarded them scowled, holding his hands up at his sides in surrender and gesturing toward the broken wheel. It wasn't hard to piece together what had happened, and I nodded toward the others.

"Let's get that wheel fixed so these nice folks can get on with their day then, huh?"

Porter and Wes nodded, both heading to work on the wagon, though with the robot it was quick work. I never asked the man or his family for anything in exchange for the work, but the woman told me they had come from the direction we were planning to go. She warned us of treacherous swamps. The family was kind enough to offer us several five-gallon jugs of water for our help. After a half hour, we had them on their way, and off we went toward Tulsa with the robot as our guide.

"Well, they were a cheerful bunch," Porter said, casting eyes back toward the wagon as it rumbled off in the opposite direction down the road.

I nodded, glancing down toward the robot, who walked awkwardly beside us.

"Robot, how much longer to Tulsa?"

The robot tittered absently, the lights along its chest blinking.

"Tulsa is 170 miles away. It will take us approximately seven days to ride there on horseback."

"Seven days? Fuck. We'll have to set up camp again tonight, then. It's a good thing we just restocked in Nevada. We wouldn't've had enough supplies to get us through a seven-day ride. That water was lucky too."

The others nodded, raising their hands to shield their faces as we reached the crest of another hill and the sun glared across the prairie. It was hot that day, and the further we rode, the less progress it seemed like we were making. Whatever route the robot had chosen for us was apparently less passable now than it had been when it was programmed.

Now the road it suggested lay scattered with dead cars, all of which nestled within the overgrown jungle that still seemed to be trying to swallow it up.

"I think we're lost, boss," Wes said quietly, taking a swig from a flask that he and Porter passed between them. I rolled my eyes.

"We can't be lost. We have a robot." I reached down, gesturing for the robot to lead the way.

"Maybe we should've let it update in Nevada like it wanted to. I don't even think it's takin' us the right direction." Wes's uncertainty wasn't helping me keep a level head.

"Lionel, you recognize any of this?"

Our horses leaped a narrow dry creek that cut the earth in half before us. The robot barely made it as it tried its best to clamber after us.

"Um...kind of? Keep your eye out for a big-ass river. Wraps around a few times. Locals call it Dragon's Pass. Tulsa's on the other side. It's just crossin' the damned thing that's the trouble. How's that new mount o' yours feel about water?" Lionel sucked on the flask as he rode, nodding in the direction he'd referenced.

"I got no idea, now that you mention it. In fact, I really don't know anything about her so far, aside from the fact she's trained to neck rein and doesn't like her feet bein' picked up."

It was evening already by the time we could hear the river in the distance, and as the sun set through the jungle, I made the decision to camp by the bank for the night.

"Why are we so close to the bank? Ain't you worried about gators?" Lionel nodded toward the fresh slides along the sandy shore. I shook my head, gesturing up toward the higher prairies above us.

"Hell, no. I'd take a gator over a hippo any day. We camp up in the prairies above the water, and the hippos will go up and graze right by our tents. It's much safer being down here. Trust me."

Lionel groaned.

"I forgot about the hippos."

Porter and I shook our heads.

"Lionel, you've been in that cozy little town too long. Hippos are the least of your problems in The Nothin'. Ain't no soldiers out here to keep you safe."

While the others set up camp, I walked the perimeter, making note of anything suspicious I saw along the way. All I found was a signpost hammered into the ground some twenty feet up the hill. I decided it could have been anything, something left over from another camp or a grave marker. I let my suspicions rest and headed back, settling in beside the fire.

"So, Lionel, tell me about yourself. Why were you in Nevada?"

Lionel laughed, grinning a bit before a solemn expression crossed his face.

"Oh, you know the story. I stayed fer a girl. The best girl. The perfect girl. We had everythin' in common, we got along, and the way we met? It was like we were in a goddamn fairytale. I asked her to marry me, gave her a ring I made and everything...and uh...we stayed like that for a while, all peaceful like. I got clean, found work in the mine. She worked at the cafe..." He trailed off for a moment, looking down so no one could see his eyes.

"So what happened?" Porter asked, motioning for him to go on with the bit of cooked meat she held in her hand.

I gave her a look, but it was too late, and Lionel's voice was already ebbing back through the dark.

"One day, she woke up, made me a cup of coffee...and uh...and left. I never saw her again."

He looked out into the jungle for a moment, one hand smoothing back his greasy hair. Then, with a rather awkward nod to us all, he rose and shuffled away toward his tent. Porter and I looked at each other, shoulders shrugging a bit. It wasn't a good feeling, remembering the things that tore us apart. Sometimes, however, it was necessary.

The night moved on slowly as one by one, familiar faces rose and moved away toward their beds. As always, Porter was the last to sit with me, her shoulders slumped, a cocky smile on her lips as she teased me about my hair. Sure, it was getting long and scruffy, but I rolled my eyes, kicking at her nearest boot playfully as the fire turned to embers between us.

Eventually, she fixed me with a look I couldn't read, and I tilted my head.

"What's goin' on in there?" I asked softly, pointing to her head beneath her messy bun and the tan hat she crammed on over it. She narrowed her eyes, as if my question was a challenge. But something changed, like I was watching a wall come down.

"Nothin'...I just..." She hesitated, glancing toward her tent where Tatiana slept, as if she was worried she might wake and hear her talk. "I...I worry is all. I mean I got the only three people in the whole world here I care about...I worry every goddamn day something might happen to Tatiana...to my dad...to you..."

I shook my head, and reached across to grab her elbow for a minute. She didn't shake me off, but she gave me a look.

"Ain't nothin' gonna happen, okay?"

Before I could even finish my sentence, she'd tossed her hat at me.

"Don't fuckin' say that, for fuck's sake. Don't you know any time someone says 'Nothin's gonna happen,' somethin' fuckin' happens?"

I rolled my eyes, glancing away just in time for a dark shadow to flit through the jungle to my left. I reached for my weapon, but I wasn't fast enough. Suddenly, through the underbrush, a lasso spun through the air. I yelled out a warning, Porter dove for her gun belt, the horses reared and whinnied where they were tied, and more figures snagged their lead ropes, shoving them back toward the river. I heard shots, but I couldn't tell if they were mine or theirs, and my gun had been knocked from my hand. Then as the lasso looped around my ankles and tightened around the leather of my boots, I fell backward and cracked my head on a rock by the fire. Everything in the night turned black.

■

I woke up gasping for breath as if I had been having a night terror. I didn't know where I was. All that I could see was the dark canopy stretching into the sky above me.

"Porter?" I called, reaching for my throbbing head as I rolled onto my elbows. I couldn't even see the glow of the lanterns around the perimeter of our camp. I didn't know how far they'd dragged me. I blinked away the tears from my eyes, pushing myself up. Finally I was able to comprehend the scene. Bodies of the horse thieves lay around me.

Dark blood covered every surface I could see—tree bark, fern leaves, and my own tawny pants and shirt too. I had no idea what had happened to the thieves. Some had bullet holes between their eyes; others had slit throats.

I stumbled away and half slumped against a tree, when I heard more gunshots in the dark. I grappled for my belt, but my weapon was gone, surely lost somewhere in the underbrush during whatever the hell had happened in the jungle that night. I wasn't as far away as I thought, and by the time I had made it back, Lionel was grappling with a man near the horses. Wes was pinned against a fallen tree near the river bank. I rushed to help as he got loose, pistol-whipping the man and shoving him off down the riverbank.

"Sharkey! What the hell happened to you?!" He grabbed me by the sides of my face, but I shoved him away, grappling for his shirt and shaking him to get his attention.

"Where's Porter, Wes?! *Where's Porter?*"

He looked away, shaking his head and pointing a trembling hand into the dark. I didn't understand, but I ran as fast as I could, leaping over fallen logs, and stumbling into the unknown. I don't know what I expected, but it certainly wasn't been what I found.

I saw Tatiana first, half naked, clothing torn and draped over her bare, blood-smeared thighs. She had been left like that, trembling in the dirt clearing where the horse thieves had taken her. I didn't need to be told what they had done to her. I already knew, and I think that's why I didn't try to stop what happened next. Porter's screams drew my eyes, but they weren't screams of pain, and the sounds that followed were worse. There was no mistaking the sound of throats being slit, the gurgle of air sucked through torn flesh, blood rushing over parted lips, the last wails echoing into the night.

Porter had one by the back of his hair, shoved down onto his knees, and she wasn't slitting his throat, no, not just yet. She had his pants down, and the bit she was working her knife through was obvious. I looked around at the bodies of the horse thieves that lay scattered around her as the last man fell, mangled, into the pool of blood and dirt at her feet. Suddenly the jungle was very quiet, and I watched Porter as she crossed and fell to the ground at Tatiana's side, arms pulling her trembling body to her chest. She was alive, but I knew that she would never be the same.

"Porter...it's over...let's get her back to camp." I stepped closer, but the dagger still clutched in Porter's blood-slicked hands turned toward me, her wild eyes searching over my face like she didn't know who I was. I raised my hands, movements slow and calculated as I approached.

"It's okay...it's okay...it's me," I whispered, pulling Tatiana carefully from Porter's arms and lifting her up against my chest. I wasn't the strongest man, but I could carry her back. I could manage that much. Porter walked beside me, breaths shaky, her blade clenched in her fist. We gathered the horses and left the bodies scattered through the forest that night. We took their weapons and the bullets in their chambers and left them out to rot.

By the time we made it back to camp, the others had dragged the remaining bodies into the river. Wes looked up, trying to figure out what had happened as I carefully lowered Tatiana into a chair beside the fire. Porter had already grabbed a blanket and worked at wrapping it around her wife's body. I shook my head, telling Wes everything he needed to know.

The preacher stepped out of the dark, cleaning the blade of his knife that he held in his hand.

"Hell is empty," he whispered, looking back and forth between his daughter and Tatiana with a deep frown on his face.

"All the devils are here."

CHAPTER FOURTEEN

ONE LAST RIDE

ICKY WOKE TO SEVEN SHOTS IN THE DARK, HAND grabbing for his weapon as he pushed himself out of his tent and into the clearing. From the hill, he could see the glow of the city far below him stretching out into the distance. Others stirred from their tents, peeking out with tired eyes and tousled hair.

"Everything okay, Ricky?" Jon asked, hand on his holstered gun.

Ricky shook his head, looking back out over the city bellow, but it was Crystal's call that drew his eyes.

"Ricky!" She gasped, stumbling from her tent and clutching at his arms, panic in her gaze.

"Where's Kent?" And it was all that needed to be said. Ricky took off toward his horse so fast that neither of them could stop him. He swung into his saddle and went tearing off down the hill with his heart in his throat and his hand on the grip of his weapon. He had never been so afraid in his life, not even when faced with death, torture, or any avenue of pain in between. Even as he rode, dread settled over him. The gunshots had stopped, and a quiet that was more terrifying than any noise he could imagine crept through the abandoned Nevada streets.

As fast as he was, he had not been fast enough. Ricky's horse slid to a stop in front of the coffee house, dust kicking up around his hooves, and when he stumbled from his panting horse, he pushed past the soldiers who stepped out into the street to stop him. It was the only storefront where soldiers had gathered. One shook his head, another scowled before he charged at Ricky, hands clutching over his shoulders. No force in the universe could have stopped him though, and he shoved the first one hard against a table, rushing past into the dull neon light the sign outside scattered through the broken glass of the door. He stood, staring down over the lifeless body of Kent Watson and the crushed French press that lay crumpled in his hand.

"Hey!" one of the soldiers shouted, helping the other one to his feet.

"That's assault against an officer, buddy!" one of the soldiers yelled, and another stepped in behind Ricky, gesturing for him to leave the way he'd come.

Ricky stared down at the body of his best friend, not a single muscle in his body moving. The soldiers stepped closer, grabbing for his arm again. That was their second mistake. In one swift movement, he snatched the first soldier up by his collar, turned him around so his back was flush against his chest, and snapped his neck with his bare hands.

"What the fuck!" The second soldier reached for his gun, but Ricky drew his knife. With a sort of grace that only the lions displayed when they hunted, Ricky sprang forward, plunging his blade into the soldier's throat. He spun and redirected the weapon of the third soldier, his bloody hands nearly slipping off the barrel, cupped it, kicked the soldier in the groin, drew the gun back, hearing the soldier's trigger finger break, and kneed him in the face. The soldier doubled over, and Ricky shot him in the back of the head.

The fourth soldier stood there hesitating, and Ricky thrust the dagger up through his ribs, aiming for the tiny extension of cloth between the plates of his body armor. Panting and screaming into the night like a wild animal, Ricky fell to his knees, breath ragged and broken between sobs. He reached for Kent, pulling his broken body into his arms.

There were no last words, no long goodbye through gasping breath, nothing said that would be remembered. He just held him there until the sirens started, as tears streaked down the stubble on his cheeks. He finally rose, hauling Kent's body and the broken French press out into the street where his horse stood. He held him carefully in front of him on the saddle, cradling him against his chest as they rode out into the dark night one last time.

The others were out of their tents when Bean started whining, and Crystal sat on the ground beside her, stroking fingers through her red fur. Only the sound of Ricky's horse silenced her; and when he appeared over the hill, she tore from Crystal's side, whimpering and crying out at her master's feet. Ricky didn't pay her any mind this time though. He turned away from her, busy lowering Kent's body carefully to the ground.

Crystal was the first to scream, and she rushed forward, throwing her arms around Kent's shoulders as Ricky propped him carefully against the trunk of a tree nearby. The others watched, eyes wide, hearts racing, as Ricky stared into the black abyss of the jungle. He didn't say a word, even as Jon came to face him, hands clutching at his shoulders.

"Ricky, what happened?" He shook Ricky's shoulders.

In the distance, soldiers made for the hillside, electric ATVs chewing up the earth in the night.

"We gotta go, Ricky!" Jon called, shoving him back toward his horse and rallying the others. He had his own problems, like getting Clay up fast enough and onto his horse before the soldiers got to them and trying desperately not to let the man see the body lying against the tree. Ricky moved forward, dropping down to scoop Kent's body back up into his arms despite Crystal's grabbing hands and sobs of protest. It took longer than it should have for everyone to pack up their tents and mount up, and by the time they went tearing off into the countryside, the soldiers' ATVs were close behind, thankfully distracted by the remnants of the camp they'd left in their wake. Kent's gray gelding Bandit tossed his head as he galloped at Ricky's side. He didn't understand why his rider wasn't with him.

They were fast enough to lose the soldiers in the jungle, and by the time they felt it was safe to stop, the first sunlight of the day had crept along the horizon, spilling golden light through the olive green leaves.

"Ricky," Crystal sobbed, slumping off her horse and into the dirt beside it.

"We gotta stop. We gotta...we gotta bury him." She sucked in a quivering breath, unable to bring herself to look at the body that Ricky still held in front of him, one of his arms cupped gingerly over Kent's chest. He nodded though, still quiet as he pulled his horse around and slowly made his way down to stand beside her. They had stopped in a clearing, and the way that the light filled the area, it made the place look important enough for the occasion.

"This is good." Finally Ricky breathed the words, cradling Kent in his arms as he nodded toward the middle of the little field. The trees that surrounded it swayed in the gentle breeze that picked up. It was peaceful. Quiet. Kent would have complained about the sunlight, told Ricky how that much light wasn't good for a man. They dug in silence at first.

Crystal, watching from the trunk of a tree where she sat, said, "Ricky, what happened? I...I don't understand."

Ricky hid his eyes beneath the rim of his hat as he worked the shovel into the ground. He paused, turning away from the trench and stepping toward Kent's body. He had only just realized that Kent still had that broken French press in his hand, the glass cutting deep into his palm. Ricky attempted to free him of it, but his fingers were already stiff with death. He winced, clutching at his face as he was forced to turn away. Jon stepped up to finish what he'd started.

"What is that, Ricky? Tell us what happened? *What happened?*"

"Kent went back for the fucking French press. Soldiers... they're dead now..."

Crystal stared at him, mortified.

"You killed *soldiers,* Ricky?" She looked around, as if she expected them to come bursting through the forest.

He jammed the shovel into the earth.

"What was I supposed to do? They killed him!" His knees gave way and he slumped over onto his elbows in the dirt.

"They shot Kent." Ricky's hands dug trenches through his scruffy hair, hat discarded on the ground behind him.

Crystal braced herself against the tree trunk, using it to push herself up on shaky legs. She crossed toward the horses, hands reaching for the face of the gray gelding, who seemed to be searching through the dark jungle for his rider still.

"What should we do with Bandit?"

Suddenly, as Ricky sat there on his knees, staring into the face of his best friend's gray horse, he was very far away. Where he'd gone, he was twelve years old, and he sat crouched over a failing fire, hands busy adjusting charred branches till the embers stirred to life.

He looked up to the sound of horses, and giddy for Papa Shark and the others to return, he shoved himself to his feet and bounded off toward the stables. Another figure halted him, smaller hands shoving him to the side as blond pigtails danced by.

"Too slow, sucker!" Porter called, her young, gangly form darting away ahead of him as he picked himself back up to follow.

"Get back here! That's not fair!" The two jockeyed to each stand first in line to greet Papa Shark as he dismounted at the stables.

"Sir!" Ricky called, standing at a sloppy attention as a disheveled Jack stepped toward them. He seemed distracted, and he didn't greet them right away.

"Get him down," he was saying, gesturing to the only other rider, the preacher, Tim Sharp, who had returned with him. Tim had one hand clutched over a bloody rag and held it up over one of his eyes. *Something wasn't right*, Ricky thought. *Where were the rest of the scrappers?* Papa Shark had left with dozens of riders. As Ricky watched, Tim helped a boy not much younger than himself down from the back of a scrawny gray horse and onto the ground before them. Finally, Jack called for Ricky, as Porter rushed to her father's side.

"Daddy! Daddy? Are you okay? What happened to your eye?" She pulled his sleeve as he tended to the eye he had lost. Ricky wanted to see, but Jack reached for his arm, kneeling down in front of him on one knee as Porter and Tim moved away from him.

"Ricky...c'mere," Jack said, gesturing to the shivering child beside him.

"This here's Kent. Now, you know how Porter's in charge of making sure Sharkey stays safe once he's born? Well this here's your charge now, okay? His parents got killed in the raid. He's your responsibility now, you hear me?"

Ricky nodded firmly, looking over the smaller boy.

"Yes, sir."

"Good boy." Jack nodded and moved away, leaving the three children in the stable yard.

Porter tried desperately to follow her father, but he shooed her away, ensuring her that he would be all right. She turned back to join the boys with a huff.

"What're we s'posed to do with him? Look how scrawny he is! There's no way we can play scrappers and monkeys with him. Maybe we can play plague, but he's gotta be the one who's dying. I'll be a soldier!"

A devilish grin played over her lips as she grabbed for the wooden pistol in her belt.

"Back, you disgusting infested human!"

She held her weapon with both hands and braced her feet, taking her best fighting stance.

Ricky frowned, shoving her away and turning the boy in the opposite direction by his shoulders.

"Fuck's sake, Porter. He doesn't wanna play plague! His family just got killed. Come on, kid. I was just settin' up my camp down by the river. You can stay there with me. I *was* staying up in Jack's house, but he and Mama fight all the time, and she's about to have a baby, so she gets all the extra attention. But I'll look out for you. Are you hungry? I can cook ya somethin' on the fire."

"Fine, whatever. I am gonna go see if my dad's all right." Porter shook her head and ran off into town, leaving the two boys standing there in the street.

"Come on," Ricky prompted again, this time reaching for the other's hand and leading him down the grassy slope across the street. The river ran slowly that evening, her voice quiet, as the two boys settled down by the little fire Ricky had built. It wasn't much, but Kent seemed to enjoy the gentle crackle of the logs. He hadn't said anything yet, but Ricky was patient, watching him as he told stories about old Jack, the town of Lawrence they called home, and the war that was starting and how they'd probably both have to fight in it when they were old enough. Finally, as Ricky stuck a sausage onto the end of a stick and tucked it against the flames, Kent spoke.

"Thanks for, ya know, helpin' me out."

Ricky tilted his head, grinning sheepishly.

"Well, Jack said so, but even if he hadn't, I would've done it anyways. From now on, it's just you and me, okay?"

"How come?"

That one took Ricky a moment, and he shrugged.

"Well, I don't really have any friends except for Porter. And she's a pain in the ass." He laughed at his own joke, snorting a little before he went on. "And you seem like fun. What's your horse's name?"

Kent glanced back toward the stable where his scrawny gray horse stood.

"Oh, that's Bandit. Mom was gonna get me a dog too. I was gonna name it Bean because I love coffee so much, but Dad said that was stupid and then, well..." He looked away, rubbing the back of his neck and moving his mop of brown hair out of his face. Ricky fixed him with confused eyes, prodding the sausage on a stick a little too roughly and topping the end of it with ash.

"What the hell is *coffee*?"

Kent's eyes went wide and he lunged for his backpack, shuffling around in it until he pulled out a crumpled bag full of coffee grounds.

"You're tellin' me you ain't never had coffee before?! Do you have a pot for water and a cup? Let me make you some. It's the best damned drink you'll ever taste! My family, we had a coffee farm. That's why we were at the market today."

The boys both smiled at each other as Ricky darted away to grab the cooking supplies he had stored away in his tent. It was all part of his plan to be self-sufficient.

As the coffee brewed, Ricky looked up from it.

"Let's do it."

Kent raised his eyebrows.

"Do what?"

"Let's get a dog." Ricky said. "An' name it Bean."

As Ricky took the first sip of coffee, his eyes lit up, and some kind of serious expression flickered over his young face. Kent almost looked concerned, like Ricky wouldn't like it.

"Did I put too much sugar in it?" He asked, reaching for the cup, but Ricky kept it away from him, sipping at it again.

"No, it's...what the heck is this stuff?"

"It's coffee, silly. Ya like it?"

Ricky gave him back the cup, asking for more with just his eyes as he nodded furiously.

"I love it! Though now that ya say it, maybe there was too much sugar, or maybe too much milk. Or not enough milk? Hell, I don't know. But I will tell you what, Kent. Someday I'm gonna make the perfect cup of coffee."

Kent snorted, shaking his head as he poured him another serving.

"You're crazy. But I sure hope I'm there to see it."

Ricky fixed him with a curious look, grinning.

"Of course you will be. Where else would you be?"

■

Ricky returned to the clearing, his shoulders heavy with the weight of everything he'd lost. He shook his head, eyes cast toward the hole that he'd dug and the fresh dirt on his boots.

"We'll take the horse, we can use him to haul supplies." He waved a hand dismissively.

"Somebody help me with him."

As they lowered Kent down into the ground, Bean whined, pawing at the raised earth where the hole began, dancing around the edge as if she wanted to leap in and stir him from his slumber.

"Come on, girl...I know...it's okay...it's okay." His breath caught in his chest when he tried to speak, and with gentle hands he coaxed the dog back while the others turned shovels of dirt back over Kent's still form. Crystal sobbed, and although Ricky never tried to comfort her, she still took shelter at his side.

"What do you say?" Jon asked, swiping his hat from his head and rubbing a hand over his face. You could tell he had been crying, but he wasn't the type to make a scene.

Clay looked on, confused, as if he didn't really understand what was happening.

"You say goodbye," Ricky said softly, staring down over the mound where his best friend lay.

"You say goodbye."

CHAPTER FIFTEEN

A GAME OF DICE

WE RODE THE LAST FEW DAYS TO TULSA IN relative silence and camped quietly, without discussing what had happened that night at all. And even though Porter did her best to pretend like everything was okay, she walked on eggshells whenever Tatiana would duck out of their tent to join us at the fire.

Wes tried to keep things light, joking with Lionel as we passed a joint between us, while the preacher seemed more solemn than ever, muttering things into his bible as he sketched verses along the bindings. Every once in a while, I would catch Porter watching Tatiana, and when Tatiana couldn't see, Porter looked at her with so much pain in her eyes.

When Tulsa finally crested on the horizon and we could see the red barn and the farmhouse where Lionel claimed that his friends lived, I allowed the others to ride ahead of me so that I could watch each one as they passed by me. I think something in me needed to confirm they were all still there, and only afterward could I find even a moment of peace. Even still, I felt a heaviness in my chest each time I took a breath, like something inside me had been broken, and this time I knew for certain I would never be who I was.

"Jordan! Holy hell kid, you grew three feet since I saw you last!" I looked up from under my hat when I heard Lionel's voice, and the sight that greeted me made my breath catch in my throat. There in front of those red barn doors stood a girl I would never forget. She wasn't anything special really: dark almond-shaped eyes, light brown skin, and straight black hair that fell below her waist. She was wearing a simple red dress and had an apron messily tied around her waist. She was waving, and I watched as the others dismounted and allowed her to help their horses into their stalls.

"I was hopin' you'd turn up again someday, Uncle Lionel. Hell, we thought you were dead."

She was grinning when she saw me, a curious expression shifting over her round face as she tilted her head to one side. I suddenly felt like a horse at auction.

"You comin'? We got plenty of room for your horse too." She motioned toward the barn doors, and I caught myself with my mouth open a bit, snapping my jaw shut as I swung down off my saddle.

"Um, yeah, thanks. Sorry. Name's Sharkey, by the way. Me and mine are headin' to Dallas...I appreciate you lettin' us restock here." I cast my eyes back toward the robot, who had come to stand at my side, and you couldn't miss the way that Jordan tensed at the sight of it.

I offered her a handshake, but she ignored it, casting her eyes back toward Lionel. Her mother came out of the house nearby to greet us. She too had seen the robot now, though, and both of them stared at the motionless shape of it beside me.

"I hope you don't think you are bringing that thing inside. Those things are dangerous," the girl said angrily, folding her arms over her chest.

The robot tittered, tilting its metallic face.

"I am forbidden from harming humans," it explained cheerfully.

Jordan's mother, a tall and equally beautiful woman whose resemblance to her daughter faltered only with the addition of gray streaks in her black hair, stepped forward, her voice stern.

"Hush, Jordan. These are our guests, and they will be welcomed into our home. *All* of them. It's wonderful to meet you, Sharkey. My name is Anabeth."

Jordan smirked, muttering under her breath.

"Sharkey?"

I cleared my throat, adjusting my shoulders awkwardly.
"Please...call me Cortez."

Porter raised her brows, grinning as she and Wes exchanged knowing glances and prodded each other with their elbows.

"Cortez," they mocked together as we all filed into the farmhouse. It was quaint, and there certainly wasn't enough room for all of us. I'd hoped we wouldn't be staying long enough to need beds for the night though. I tried to catch Porter's eye, nodding for her to meet me in the corner of the room.

She stepped up to my side, still wagging her brows like she knew something I didn't.

"You totally like that girl," she teased, and I gave her a look.

"What are you, twelve? Who cares?" I nodded toward the robot, who was standing awkwardly at the head of the table.

"Keep that thing outta trouble, all right? They don't seem to like it too much."

"You'll have to excuse the mess," Anabeth interrupted, shuffling a few articles of clothing from a nearby seat and tucking them away in a closet near the back of the room.

"My husband is very ill. I haven't had much time to clean."

She offered the group a smile much too kind for having endured such things, and she gestured toward the table in the middle of the room.

"Please join us for dinner. We don't have much, but we have more than you I reckon."

We obliged without argument, all hats removed and set into our laps as the preacher called for hands to join. Jordan smirked when she rested her palm over mine, and I lifted my brows, listening to the old man talk.

"O Lord, who lends me life, lend me a heart replete with thankfulness."

It was one of the simplest things he'd ever read from that book, but somehow it was perfect. He'd told me when I was little that the most meaningful line his lord had ever written was "He died." He meant the death of King Lear, a man the preacher spoke of often. Still, I was having a hard time believing that the preacher's god was looking out for any of us anymore.

"So," Anabeth said, setting a pot of stew on the table between us and sorting through a pile of mismatched ceramic bowls.

"I know you are all friends of Lionel's here, but how'd you all meet? Last I heard Lionel was out of the game and he was settlin' down with a girl in Nevada."

Lionel made a motion for her to be quiet, but it was too late. I cut in, holding a hand up.

"Game?"

"No need to get into any of that."

Lionel waved another hand dismissively, laughing awkwardly as a quiet settled over the table.

Porter's eyes were on me as I persisted.

"No, no, please. Go on." It wasn't a suggestion, and Anabeth was the first to notice.

"Lionel was once the most wanted arms dealer in the Midwest. It's a wonder he ever got *into* Nevada, let alone out of it without a rope around his neck." Her eyes were unapologetic between the ladle of soup she held and the frowning face of Lionel across the table.

I forced a laugh through my nose, slamming my fists down over the countertop as I pushed myself to my feet.

Lionel opened his mouth to speak, but I shook my head, pointing to the door. Muffled voices started the second I ducked out into the still night, and as soon as Lionel joined me I rounded on him, pressing him back against the side of the house with one hand braced beside his neck.

"Do you have any idea how much danger you put my people in by keepin' that from me?"

Lionel grabbed for my shoulders, shaking his head.

"I'm sorry, Sharkey. It was never like that. I just, I didn't want to be that man anymore, and I thought that if I just pretended to be someone else, I could have a shot at life again. Man, I...I have never met anyone like you guys. I've never had a family like that."

I sighed, taking his shoulders up in firm hands.

"I understand why you did it, Lionel. Trust me, I wish I could be someone else too. But these people are all I have left, and I gotta put them first."

He seemed to know what I meant, and his face dropped, a wince overtaking the hopeful smile he'd had on before.

"Sharkey, come on, man. I had your back when those horse thieves showed up, didn't I? You can count on me."

I didn't want to turn him away. I didn't want to be the man in his life who he'd grow to hate. But I had to do the hard thing that day.

"Were you the one who saved me that night?"

"What? Nah, I didn't know where you went. I was tryin' to keep those assholes away from the horses."

I shook my head, reaching up to run my fingers through the hair under my hat.

"Who the hell saved me? Well, regardless, Lionel, you gotta stay here, all right? I'm sorry. I just can't risk it, not after what happened to Tatiana. If you've got a bounty that big on your head, we won't make it far."

Lionel hung his head, a frown visible through his stubble.

"I understand, boss. I hope you guys make it through that portal, all right?"

"All right."

There was a touching moment that passed between us, where he held my shoulder in his hand and our eyes met in the evening light. Then we ducked away into the house.

By the time we returned to the dinner table, everyone was laughing, and Porter was in the middle of recounting exactly how we'd stumbled upon the robot, specifically the part where my pony had thrown me over its head. She went quiet when she saw the way my eyes were suddenly far away, but I smiled, nodding for her to continue. I never minded hearing stories that made me sad. I would forever be the man who'd gotten his father killed, who'd been banished from his hometown by his mother, who'd stood by while a woman and a boy who was possibly his own were eaten alive by lions. And until the day I died, Buddy's death would always be with me.

"So, *Cortez*," Jordan said, and it made me grin around the spoonful of soup I had just shoveled into my mouth.

"There ain't much to do around this old farm, but right down the road there's this shitty little bar. You up for it?" It was assumed that she was inviting everyone, but her dark eyes never left my own as she pushed herself up from the table.

Porter gave me a passing look that I ignored, and the lot of us, minus the robot and Jordan's mother, who stayed back to entertain it, made our way down the road on foot, the light from the setting sun painting us gold and silhouetting us against the countryside.

As we walked, Jordan watched me, and I watched Tatiana, who walked hand in hand with Porter. I knew that she hated the expression on my face, but I couldn't help it. Every time I saw her, her red painted lips, her dark skin, her curly hair bouncing over her shoulders, I was reminded of the image of her crumpled and broken on the ground beside the slain bodies of the men who had violated her. It was enough to drive me crazy with rage.

Jordan didn't know the story, but she never asked, and I always appreciated that about her.

As we stepped into the bar's interior, an old guitar started up in a corner—and my eyes met Jordan's again. I knew exactly how that night would end. We did all of the things that were expected of us, all of the things you do when you know what something is, and what something can never be. She laughed at all of my jokes, touched my hand when it came close across the table. We played dice, and I let her win, and she knew it.

We danced when the music got slow, and somehow, even
though we both knew every single step was part of the play, even
the one she missed on purpose so she could stumble into my
arms, that night with Jordan was more real than anything I had
ever experienced.

Porter and Tatiana left first, and the preacher and Wes took
shots until Wes slumped over the table and the preacher had to
take him out on his shoulder. Jordan watched me as I sat back
down across from her, my hand resting over her leg beneath
the table.

"So, Jordan, what're you all about? I can't quite figure you.
What're you doing in this town in the middle of nowhere?"

She lifted her eyebrows, rouged lips resting over the edge of
her glass for a moment before she answered.

"What? This isn't enough?" She smiled, her fingers tracing
over the rough knuckles of my fingers.

"Sorry my life doesn't fit the exciting narrative you'd expect of
someone my caliber, but I think this place is perfect." She kind of
looked around for a minute while she said it, and somehow the
certainty behind her answer was everything.

We spent the night in a room upstairs, and in the morning,
as my lips pressed gentle shapes into her bare back beside me, I
asked her to come with me.

"This is why you're so unhappy, Sharkey," she yawned back,
watching me over her shoulder.

"You keep searching for this moment where everything that's
happened so far will make sense, but it won't come. You just
keep going until you die. So no, I am not gonna come with you.
I am not gonna let you whisk me away on an adventure. I am
gonna stay here, in this little town in the middle of nowhere, and
I am gonna be happy."

I laughed, nodding as she reached up to trail her fingers down
the stubble of my cheeks.

"My dad always said you should never be afraid of

anything...cuz nowadays you either do it right and have the time of your life or you die. And if you die then you don't gotta worry about it anymore." She smiled, and I will never forget the impression that smile left on me, even as we dressed in silence and I kissed her without saying goodbye.

It wasn't until I returned to the farm that I became aware something wasn't right. It was early enough still that the others slept, but Porter had already saddled our horses and stood waiting at the hitching post beside them, taking long drags of a cigarette.

As I approached, she pushed off with her shoulders and came to face me, eyes cast down into the dirt at my feet as she clutched my shoulder to turn me away toward our mounts.

"Porter, what's goin' on?" I glanced over my shoulder at Jordan, who offered me a simple smile and ducked inside. I never saw her again.

Porter took an unsteady breath, and I could see the unrest in her face.

"We gotta go, Sharkey, before my dad and Tatiana wake up. It's the only way I can keep them safe."

I stared at her for a long moment, mouth open, but I knew she was right. So instead, I took her face in my hands, and I held her chin so she couldn't look away.

"Porter...are you sure about this? The portal...we might not be able to come back."

She shook her head, casting her eyes away as a tear streaked down her cheek. I didn't try to brush it away, afraid that if I brought attention to it, she'd lose that tiny bit of control that she clung to. Instead, I nodded toward the house as I turned away to grab my horse from the hitching post.

"Go wake Wes," I ordered softly. "Let's get goin'."

She nodded firmly, hanging on by a thread as she left to gather Wes from the stables, where he'd spent the night. She was careful not to make too much noise as she passed by the house, where

Tatiana and the preacher slept peacefully. I wondered if they'd ever forgive her or me for allowing her to make this decision in the first place. But somewhere deep inside I knew there was no other way to guarantee their safety, and I understood exactly why Porter did what she did that day.

CHAPTER SIXTEEN

CONTROL

ICKY AND HIS PEOPLE RODE ON ACROSS THE
countryside with holes in their hearts where Kent had
been. They never discussed the state that Ricky was in,
but every one of them had seen a darkness in his eyes
that scared them. But they weren't aware how truly unhinged
he had become. By the time they came across the wagon where
Sharkey and his group had stopped to help with a broken wheel,
something horrible had begun.

A woman screamed. That alone was enough to make Ricky
kick his horse into a gallop and charge through the line of trees
onto the dirt road. Jon could have stopped him, but Clay was so
scared that he was starting to panic, and everything happened
so quickly. It took seconds for Ricky to swing down off his
horse, realize what was happening, and rush forward to pull the
man off his wife. Two children cowered in the wagon, crying
out for their mother, who lay crumpled, bloody, and beaten at
Ricky's feet.

Something snapped in him then, as he held that man by
the scruff of his shirt. Not even Ricky understood why he was
beating that man. At one point, when the man was no longer
dangerous to anyone, he should have stopped, but he didn't.

"Ricky! Stop!" Crystal sobbed, and only then, as her voice
sounded to him like it was very far away, was he able to stop. His
fist sat there in the air for a while, his eyes unfocused, staring
down into the bloodied pulp of the man, who was now dead.

Finally the woman screamed again, and Ricky was able to
stand on shaking legs to face her.

"You can...you can come with us. We'll keep you safe."

The others stared at him with wide, traumatized eyes, but the
woman shook her head, still sobbing and clutching at the body of

her slain husband. Ricky cleared his throat with an expression on his face that no one could identify. He said, "Take some of their supplies. We'll need 'em to get to Tulsa."

Without saying anything else, he turned away, mounted his horse, and walked off down the road, leaving what he'd done far behind him.

After the others gathered up several gallons of water, hay, and canned food and packed it onto Bandit's saddle, it was miles and hours past nightfall until anyone spoke.

"Are you okay?" Crystal asked softly, riding on Ricky's right, her soft eyes watching him in the moonlight.

Ricky shook his head, staring forward for a long time.

"No Crystal...I don't think I am."

Crystal looked away, one hand moving down to rest on the neck of her mount as they rode and only the distant sound of gunfire stirred them from their quiet mourning.

"Sharkey?" Crystal whispered, looking back over her shoulder as the others joined them on the crest of the hill. Looking down over the sloping meadow, they could see the forest and the glow of Sharkey's lanterns.

"Isn't it always?" He muttered.

"All of you, *stay*. I will check on Sharkey."

Ricky cast one last glance over his remaining people before galloping down toward the tree line. By the time he dismounted and swung down into the underbrush with his pistol drawn, Sharkey had been driven away from the others and Ricky found him lassoed and unconscious at the feet of several horse thieves.

"Leave him! Get the women!" one called, ordering two others back into the forest and toward the sound of Porter and Tatiana in the distance. Ricky pushed himself up against a tree, listening, watching as the pair moved away and the others moved to grab for Sharkey's body. Ricky charged forward, grabbing one from behind and breaking his neck before firing off several rounds at the others. By the time he finished, bodies of the horse thieves lay scattered around the little clearing.

He brushed himself off and stared down over Sharkey for a long moment. Then falling down onto his knees beside him, he reached into the boy's front pocket and snatched a joint. One finger strayed to brush a few strands of his messy red hair away from his eyes. His brow was smeared with blood, and he looked like he'd already been through hell before the attack.

"Ya know, I underestimated you, kid. You're one tough son of a bitch..."

He stepped away from him and ducked quietly into the forest to see if the others were okay. Unfortunately he was too late to help Tatiana, and by the time he saw Porter through the trees, she'd already killed the last man, so he left before any of them even knew he was there.

Crystal smiled when he returned, having watched from the top of the hill as he protected a man he mostly despised.

"You did good," she whispered, reaching out across the space between their horses to rest a hand on his forearm. Ricky shook his head, eyes cast away from her to the place where Sharkey lay.

"Not good enough. Nothin' will ever be good enough, Crystal."

They camped in the field that night, under the wide open sky and the swath of stars. Ricky couldn't remember the last time he hadn't had Kent there beside him at the firepit, teasing him about one thing or another, going on about autumn or how it was too hot for his sensitive skin. At one point Clay looked up and pointed into the sky.

"Look Ricky! A shooting star!" Kent would have loved that.

For hours, he sat alone, with one hand on Bean's back and a frown on his face. For the first time, he didn't bother to unpack his coffee, and he went to sleep that night without his tent, just Kent's saddle under his head. ■

When morning finally came and Ricky stirred from his restless sleep, there was a moment where he forgot, and for the rest of his life, that moment, the one that only came in the first few seconds of awake, would haunt him. He rolled over, expecting to see Kent's face; and when he didn't, everything came crashing back over him.

For the second time in his life, he left his coffee in his saddlebag and stirred the others from their tents without breakfast.

"Come on guys...we gotta get going...I don't know where Sharkey's heading, an' I don't want to lose him."

The others complied with only quiet protests offered, a huff here, a sideways glance there, given in the morning light as they saddled and mounted and headed off into the countryside rubbing sleep from their eyes. It didn't take them long to realize that Sharkey was heading toward Tulsa, but they were lagging considerably behind, and by the time they followed their tracks to the red barn on the hillside, Sharkey and his people were assumed to be far away.

Ricky stopped some feet from the door, eyes cast toward the barn and the many sets of hoofprints, accompanied by the robot's, that led away into the countryside. He didn't think anything of the familiar black mare who still stood in the barn. He should have recognized her. Any of them should have. How many times had they watched the preacher saddle Juliet? A hundred? A thousand?

Instead, he stepped up to the house and knocked on the door, unprepared for who would greet him only moments later.

"Ricky?" Tatiana stared at him with wide eyes through the open doorway, her dark brows lifting and her face covered with tears. One hand came to rest over her parted lips. Ricky stared at her for too long, and before he could even open his mouth to reply, Crystal had pushed past him and thrown her arms around Tatiana, pulling her into a tight hug. They cried together, though for different reasons.

"What are you doing here? I...I don't understand!"

Tatiana spoke with a voice that had been strained by sobs, and it didn't take Ricky long to realize something wasn't right.

He nodded to the preacher, who sat at the table, as he stepped inside and to the two women who presumably lived there. One of them, an older woman with kind eyes, approached to gesture welcomingly toward the deeper corners of the house.

"Please, come in. Friends of Tatiana's are friends of ours." Her daughter looked up angrily at Ricky. She snorted as she pushed past him out the door. All she had to say was muttered under her breath.

"I'll water your horses."

Ricky didn't question her attitude, nor did he have much to say to the woman who had offered them refuge in her home.

Tatiana and Crystal still stood arm in arm by the doorway, but Ricky was growing increasingly impatient with the pleasantries everyone else seemed too keen to share.

"Where's Sharkey? Why isn't he with you?"

"Where's Sharkey?" Tatiana wiped away the tears from her cheeks so that the stern expression she wore next looked more serious.

"What do you mean where's Sharkey? What the hell are you doing here?"

Ricky cursed under his breath, heading for the window and tearing back the curtain so he could peer outside. It wasn't clear if he had ignored her question or if he hadn't heard it in the first place.

"How long of a head start does he have? When did he leave? Where was he going?"

The others exchanged worried looks, and as Tatiana stepped toward Ricky, Crystal grabbed for her arm to stop her and pulled her close. Although her voice was quiet when she tried to explain, one word was loud enough to make Ricky wince from across the room.

"Tatiana...please...it's Kent."

"Kent? What about him? Where is he?"

Ricky didn't need to be there for the rest of the story, he had relived it too many times inside his head. He turned on a heel fast enough to make them jump, startled eyes on him as he interrupted.

"We don't have time for this, Tatiana. Where the fuck is Sharkey?"

Without warning he'd grabbed for Tatiana's shoulders harder than he'd meant to, and he hadn't expected the cry that escaped her as she pulled away from him. He stared down at her, startled, apologetic, ashamed of his reaction, and curious about the way she shook now, cradled in the protective arms of her father-in-law. For the first time that he could remember, there was something like hatred on the preacher's face, and without giving him time to process what was happening, the old man dragged him into the lamplit clearing outside the door.

"Shut the fuck up." It wasn't often the preacher displayed anything but solemn contemplation, and for him to choose his own words, not God's, was rare, especially words as cruel as those. Ricky straightened his shoulders, head bowed slightly.

"Sorry, sir...I've been through a lot since I left Lawrence."

"Cry me a fuckin' river. You think I wanted to see that boy get ripped in half by a gorilla? You think I wanted to be the one to find his brother's body? I was the one who helped pull that horse off Jack, my oldest friend, cradled his crushed body in my arms. You think I wanted to hear Peggie screaming as she was ripped apart by lions? I was there when Chesser was born. I baptized him. I was the one that gave them all rites. I have witnessed worse things on this journey than in all the wars I've fought. Every one of us has been through hell, Ricky, but we don't have time to whine about it. I know what your job is. I was the one who told Mama that you'd be able to get it done, and I know that you can make it through this. I know that you are strong enough to keep him safe." He had his old hands clenched on Ricky's arms, and as he spoke, the wall that Ricky had built up for so long came crumbling down.

"Tim...I lost Kent. How am I supposed to go on without him? I don't think I can...I know I am supposed to be strong but I...I don't feel strong without him."

The preacher watched him for a long moment, processing the news of Kent's death, while his hands moved up to brace either side of Ricky's face; and when he spoke, a gentle smile graced his old lips despite the pain in his voice, his one eye gleaming in the light.

"Ambition, the soldier's virtue, rather makes choice of loss than gain which darkens him. You will prevail in your endeavor. I have faith your steadfast soul abides as long as you breathe. I chose you to guard our charge and see him home. I foresaw your ambition, and even if it meant you'd lose yourself, you'd keep fast your honor and your duty's force. I know that is a sacrifice you never saw nor thought you would endure. Now go. Ride for Dallas. You will find your way to Sharkey, and he will save us from this hell."

Ricky bowed his head, resting his forehead against the preacher's for just a moment.

"I don't feel it, Preacher, but I will do my best. I promise, for Kent, for Peggie, for Chesser and the others."

As they stood forehead to forehead, a wind that smelled like rain spiraled around them, the horses in the stable calling out a warning into the day. Ricky cast his eyes over his shoulder, one hand rising to push his hat back over his head as he turned away toward the door to the house.

He assumed that the story had come out by the time he stepped back into the yellow light the old lightbulbs on the ceiling cast across the open kitchen, judging by Tatiana's wails and the way that Crystal held her in her arms. But Ricky didn't have time for condolences either.

"Crystal, Mayra, Jon, Clay." Each head rose to meet his eye as he called their names, and several of them stepped forward obediently to face him. Ricky took a moment to watch each and every one of them, as if he was trying to make sure he would remember their faces.

"Listen to me. This is it. This is the final leg, and I can't promise any of you that we'll come back alive. You can stay here, and I won't think any less of you, all right?"

He watched them, allowing his eyes to flick between the faces that turned away from him. Crystal smiled and pressed a gentle kiss to Tatiana's forehead before pulling away and stepping to Ricky's side. Gingerly, she took his rough hand and held it carefully in her own.

"I'm not goin' anywhere but with you."

Mayra stepped up to his other shoulder, and even though she didn't have anything to say, he knew what her silence meant.

What he hadn't expected was the look on Jon's face as he closed the gap between them, one hand reaching out to rest on Ricky's shoulder.

"Ricky, we've known each other a hell of a long time. You've been like a brother to me and Clay. You've always kept us safe, fed, and clothed...and nothin' I can say to you now could come close to meaning enough. But Clay, he's all I got now, and he's real scared, Rick, and Jordan here, she's been tellin' me about some folks here who know how to take care of people like him. They can help him. Teach him things...things I never could."

Both Ricky and Jon look toward Clay together, and even as Clay bowed his head in disgrace, chubby fingers tugging at the ends of his coat, Ricky smiled.

"Take care of yourself, Jon. And Clay?" Ricky stepped around him, and although he knew better than to touch Clay, he looked him in the eye.

"Clay, I am gonna need you to take good care of Jon now, okay? That's an order. You hear me?"

Clay smiled bashfully, nodding his head, and to all of their surprise, he flung his arms around the smaller man's shoulders, pulling him into a bear hug so tight that Ricky's back popped.

"Yes, sir, Mr. Ricky. Clay will take good care of Jon."

"Let's go then, if we don't beat this storm, we may lose Sharkey's trail completely."

Ricky, Crystal, and Mayra rode out into the storm with heavy hearts, silent and together in their grief.

CHAPTER SEVENTEEN

IN THE END

"Y OU LIKED THAT GIRL A LOT, DIDN'T YOU?" PORTER
asked, watching me from her horse.

I laughed through my nose, shrugging my shoulders.

"Yeah, she was somethin', wasn't she?"

Porter looked confused, her hands clutching her reins tighter
as she jogged through the underbrush to join me.

"Then why the hell didn't you fight harder to bring her with
you?"

I knew what she was doing: trying to understand why she left
Tatiana and her father behind by trying to figure out why I did.
I shook my head, reaching out across the divide between our
mounts to rest my hand on her forearm.

"We can't take back what we did. I let her go because she
already had everything figured out, and I knew that if I stole
her from that she'd come to resent me...and you left 'em behind
because you'd rather have them resent you than die. Now you
could spend the rest of your life tryin' to figure out if you made
the right decision...but I won't let you."

And although we never said so out loud, I believe for the
first time in our lives, we both meant to tell each other "I love
you, too."

A storm had rolled down from the foothills. Lightning flashed
across the sky, thunder rumbled around us, and a torrent of rain
started next. The robot had the most difficult time clambering
over the damp rocks, and I dismounted to help it down into
the valley.

"We shouldn't be riding through this right now!" Wes said.
"We should've gone for high ground!"

A stream of water ran from his leather hat. The horses

147

threw their heads, pulling at their bits and pawing at the muddy ground.

"Don't you think I know that, Wes? But you reckon this robot's gonna make it up that path?" I gestured for Porter to take my horse. Already a stream off the rocks poured into the valley. The robot took my hand, using me to push itself up over another boulder, and despite the state of things, its voice was chipper and full of hope.

"Sharkey," it tittered, the lights on its blank white face blinking in and out of existence through the rain as it grappled over a rock ledge, bits of it crumbling away under its weight.

"My processing indicator has been active for one hundred and thirty years now. Do you think it will ever stop?"

The others looked back, dumbfounded by the robot's question and for once, I had nothing at all to say in reply. I did, however, consider the question silently while I pushed the robot forward. I wondered if there was some deeper meaning and if the robot had accidentally stumbled upon it.

Maybe it had simply begun to malfunction after all this time. I suppose we will never know.

"Sharkey, get back on your horse. I'll handle the robot. Just go! You'll be safer on your horse!" It was Wes who yelled at me through the downpour. The thunder was so loud I could barely hear him.

"No way!" I said, but before I could fight him on it further, he'd swung down from his horse and snatched the robot up and over the front of his saddle.

I am not entirely sure what happened next, whether it was the landslide that started first or the hooves of his old horse sliding down into the thick mud that sent her toppling sideways. It was more than I could process, but I reached to grab him across the sudden dark divide. The robot held onto me instead, and as I called out into the howling wind, I watched helplessly from the crest of the broken earth as the depths of the valley's innards opened up to swallow him whole.

"*Wes*!" I screamed, but he was already far beneath me, his own cries echoed by his horse, who threw her head back and went lifeless over top of his crumpled form. The storm raged on around us, Porter at my shoulder, both of us staring down into the flooding pit where Wes lay pinned beneath the dead body of his mare. Our eyes met, though every time I attempted to clear my vision to see him properly, rain flooded back down my face. I couldn't be sure whether I was crying, but my heart raced in my chest as I grappled over the edge of the pit. I wasn't about to follow him down, but Porter wouldn't have let me even if I had tried. She held me around my waist.

"Sharkey, there's nothin' we can do! There's no way down. We aren't strong enough to get the horse off...I—"

"Don't say it!"

"I saved the robot, Porter!" I threw my head back, slumping into her arms.

"I saved the fuckin' robot." I cast my eyes over the vacant face of the thing that had cost me my best friend's life, but Wes's coughs stirred me from my mourning.

"*Wes*?" I scrambled for the ledge once more, staring down into his open eyes, his half smile marred with blood and dirt.

"Sharkey! Sharkey, I...I can't feel my legs."

I opened my mouth to reply, but Porter pulled me back, hands braced over my shoulders.

"Sharkey...the horse broke his spine. He'll die slow."

I shoved her backward.

"*Shut up!*" But I knew she was right, and when her next words came through the pounding rain, I knew in my heart that this would be the point I would never return from.

"You know what you have to do, Sharkey. He'd want it to be you."

I sobbed, shifting forward until I could bury my face against the crook of her neck and her leather coat, her hands encircling me, before she handed me my own pistol.

I moved back, met her eyes, and nodded firmly. I crawled on

hands and knees until the edge of the pit crested and fell away. Wes and I looked into each other's eyes. His gaze settled on the weapon in my hand.

"Just...just close your eyes, Wes. Close your eyes for me, okay?"

He didn't, not for a long time. First he smiled as he ran his hands over the hide of his mare, tears rolling down his cheeks. Then finally, he let his lashes fall, and the expression on his young face made it look as if he had only fallen asleep. Another sob racked through my body, and it took me too long to still my hands that aimed my pistol, so when the shot finally came, not even Porter was prepared. Both of us jumped, and for what seemed like hours risking hypothermia, and for the landslide to take us too, we sat there on the edge of that pit, arms around each other.

It was still five days to Dallas. Porter and I rode, camped, ate, and slept without talking. The robot would ramble sometimes, asking questions neither of us knew the answer to, but for the most part, Porter and I didn't have anything at all to say. So I sat by the fire on the fifth night, gazing out over the hill that banked down to the towering wall of the city, and I watched as birds flew through the glow the portal cast into the darkened sky.

I thought about all of the people we had lost. I thought about my father, the brothers, my pony, Peggie and Chesser, Wes...and I wondered to myself what the hell the point of it all was.

Porter sat down beside me, her hands moving toward the flame that flickered by my boots, her tan cheeks glowing in the light that the fire threw into the jungle. She was all I had now.

"I am so sorry, Porter," I whispered, my voice hardly audible.

She looked me in the eyes. When she spoke, her voice was full of courage, and I wasn't sure how she managed it in spite of the pain she was in.

"Shut the fuck up."

It was just enough to make me smile for the first time in days, and for hours after that we sat shoulder to shoulder, gazing out over the distant Dallas spires and the crest of the portal's silver frame along the edge of the concrete wall.

■

We had prepared for some kind of armed barricade, a hundred soldiers with machine guns ready and riot shields, but as a culmination of an epic journey goes, the walk to the Dallas gate was as anticlimactic as they come.

Where is everyone? I asked myself, glancing each way down the wall as it stretched away into the distance, curving around until it vanished completely from our sight. The robot stepped forward, voice cheerful as ever as it pressed the palm of its hand into the receptacle beside the little access door before us.

"According to my records, there should be almost three million people living in Dallas, Texas."

"Yeah, so where are they?" I pushed past the robot, Porter close behind me, as the door swung open. I stared, dumbfounded, at the empty streets of the city. There were no soldiers, no bustling crowds, no storefronts full of smiling faces to welcome us into paradise. All that met us was blowing trash, the distant ruckus of monkeys who had made it over the wall and into a business nearby, and the ever-present hum of the portal, which seemed to haunt the abandoned streets of Dallas.

Something about the sheer emptiness of the city seemed to taunt us, telling us silently that all this time we could have walked in, and not a single soul would have even tried to stop us. But there was more to it than that, like a joke had been played on the world and we were the last to know. Or maybe we were the first to know. The robot followed us as we progressed through the desolate streets.

"Sharkey, Sharkey, look at this! Look at all this stuff! It's like they just up and left! Imagine what Lawrence could do with all of this!" Porter was peering through a dusty store window, and through the glass we could see shelves of food. I couldn't process anything, and I slumped into the middle of the street on my knees.

"Sharkey?" Porter was there quicker than I could have imagined, her hands on my arms, her face near my own until the edges of our hats met. She grabbed my chin in one of her hands and forced me to look up at her.

"Hey, stay with me, kid. You know I'm with you till the end no matter what, okay? You want to go through that portal? We'll go through that fucking portal."

She pushed me backward just enough to pull me out of my dissociation.

I shook my head, hand reaching for my hat and pushing it down over my back so that the gentle mist that fell around us could touch my face. I pushed myself to my feet, set my hat back over my mess of ginger hair, and set off toward the glow of the portal.

I looked up into the portal's towering face as we approached. It was huge, a massive circular frame of wires and metal that rose up far into the sky, large enough they could have sent shipping containers through it. Then as the robot stepped up and pressed its hand over the console at the portal's edge, it burst to life in a rush of silver light. It was brighter than I was expecting, the shimmering veil flickering as the wormhole made contact on the other side. Suddenly everything that had happened watched me from that portal's face, every moment not just since I left Lawrence. My entire life flashed through each wave of energy that rolled infinitely over itself into the black hole in its center. And even though I should have been filled with some innate swell of destiny's summons, fear soured my stomach.

"Porter, this is your last chance—"

"I swear to god if you tell me to stay behind, I'll fuckin' shoot you right now!"

I laughed, smiling finally as I looked ahead, my shoulders braced, both of us prepared to face whatever came next together.

"Well," I said, tugging my jacket into place.

"I got the first tab on the other side."

Porter smiled, and I don't remember how long our eyes met. Then without looking back, Porter and I stepped forward, vanishing into the portal together.

CHAPTER EIGHTEEN

OPEN DOORS

THE STORM RAGED ON, TURNING UP RICKY'S COAT and blinding him as he pushed forward through the valley. He wasn't even sure where he was going. The mud had washed away any trail that Sharkey's group had left. All that he knew was that he had to keep moving forward. He couldn't fail this quest and break faith with the preacher.

He looked back over his shoulder, searching through the torrent for the blurred shapes of Crystal and Mayra behind him.

"Stay close!" he called, but it wouldn't have made a difference, not when the earth itself gave way, trees, rock, all of it rushing forward, crumbling in front of his eyes and pulling everything it touched with it down the ragged edge of the cliff beside them. Even if he had been faster, leaped from his horse, grabbed the others somehow, it wouldn't have been enough.

Ricky's horse rolled, screaming as the side of the hill gave way, rushing over them and pulling all three riders and their mounts into a river of mud, trees, rocks, and raging water. Ricky had the foresight to push off his saddle, but suddenly the world got dark, and all he could do was call out into the crushing weight of the hill over the top of him.

Ricky woke for a second time to a gunshot, this one closer than the others had been. But by the time he came to his senses, the gunshot he'd heard felt more like a dream. He looked up to see his horse had pulled himself to his feet and stumbled, muddy but alive, toward the line of standing trees in the distance. He had his head down, his saddle skewed and his reins dragging under him. Ricky desperately tried to claw the mud away from his eyes.

"Crystal? Mayra?" Ricky choked on muddy water as he shoved rubble from his legs and chest. He winced as he stood,

154

glaring down at a bleeding wound in his leg. He looked around.
How anyone could survive, he didn't know, but his search for the
others dragged on.

"*Crystal! Mayra! Bean?*" he screamed, lightning cracking
over the darkened sky as he headed for the pile of shattered tree
trunks and boulders that had come crashing down at the bottom
of the valley. Suddenly Bean barked from the crest of the hill
they'd fallen from, and she worked her way down toward her
master on careful paws.

"Please..." he begged, hands torn and battered as he shoved
rocks aside, digging into the mud, pushing past tree branches as
he desperately searched for the others. Finally, nearly lost in the
sound of the rain, Crystal's voice called out to him.

"Crystal?!" He scrambled to her side, pulling her up and into
his arms, but it's Mayra's body that made his breath catch in
his chest.

"Ricky," Crystal sobbed, gazing over his shoulder, over the
bodies of their two dead horses half buried in rubble behind him.
Ricky saw the wound in her stomach and knew she wasn't going
to make it long.

"*No!*" Ricky sobbed, clutching her tighter, muddy, bleeding
fingers holding onto her dress as he buried his face against
her shoulder.

She pulled away, cupping his cheeks in her shaking hands.

"Ricky, it's okay. But...but I can't see where he's goin' now,
so you gotta be there with him. He can't do it without you."

"*Screw him!*" Ricky sobbed as he stared down into Crystal's
face, and she smiled the sweetest smile he had ever seen in his
life. Even then, even in pain, slumped over the body of her dead
friend, even after everything they had seen together, she could
look so untouched by The Nothing. So perfect.

"Can...can you stay with me, Ricky?" And he did. He rocked
her slowly in his arms as the rain poured down around them,
his dark hair clinging to his face. And he sang to her, he sang
to her through sobs and the crack of lightning and the thunder

that rolled through the valley. She was beautiful, and he would remember her that way.

As Ricky turned away from her body, Bandit stepped out of the woods unscathed, his saddlebags still full of supplies, and Ricky could have sworn that Kent was sitting in his saddle.

Ricky rode at a gallop for days; he never stopped. He never slept. He pushed his horse until he couldn't run anymore, then he rode Bandit for the rest of the leg. Then finally the wall of Dallas loomed before them. He and Bean walked into the rain that still fell, shielding his face when the sunlight finally broke through the clouds to cascade golden rays around them both. And like some sick joke had been played on him, the door he expected to have to fight to get through stood wide open and unguarded, welcoming him in.

Ricky stepped into the city with his head held high, steely eyes searching for the masses that he had expected to greet him with violence and misunderstanding, but they never came. He looked both ways down the long, abandoned street that stretched along the wall's interior and into the faces of the many empty shops as he moved forward toward the ominous glow of the portal light that bled into the city. There was no one there...no soldiers to stop him, no crowds to question where he'd come from.

And then, as he crossed over the threshold of the last block, the portal visible between the buildings, he could just see the outline of two familiar shapes silhouetted against it. So he'd made it. Sharkey and Porter would walk into the portal and that'd be that.

He didn't smile, but some weight lifted from his shoulders, and without much care, he looked to his right absently. That's when he saw it. A coffee shop, its OPEN sign blinking at him in the evening light. And although he wasn't entirely sure what he was expecting now, he stepped tentatively through the doors. The smell of fresh roasted beans, steamed milk, and the dust on the tables almost brought tears to his eyes. The sound of the bell rang like a voice from beyond the veil. He let his hand fall from the golden knob of the door, his eyes vacant, gazing out over the countertop and into the face of the old barista.

"What can I get ya, sir?" the man asked tiredly, and Ricky could tell that he wasn't afraid of the holstered guns on his hip or the scars on his face. That barista, with his aged gray eyes, had seen so much, and Ricky realized that no matter what happened, that man would die in this city. He probably didn't care at all what happened to him now.

Ricky stood for a long time in the doorway, framed by the golden light that pooled around him through shafts of dust, Bean sitting obediently at her master's side.

Then finally, with a certain amount of determination in his voice, he said "I'll take a coffee…"

Damaged fingers reached for the broken French press in his pocket, hardly anything more than shards now, and very carefully he sat it down over a nearby table.

"Cream or sugar?" The barista replied as if this moment was anything but extraordinary, and he shuffled about from the cabinet to the coffee machine beside him. He had probably made thousands of cups of coffee in his life. This one was no different. Pour the beans in the grinder, pour the grinds in the filter, pour the water in the machine, push the button, pour the coffee in the cup, and serve. It was simple. He did it without thinking, practiced moves, techniques he'd perfected. He knew exactly how long it took. Ricky watched him perform this simple act with such little care. And when he sat that steaming cup of coffee on the table, he did so with little grace, splashing the coffee over the side of the cup onto the tabletop.

Ricky lowered himself into the chair slowly, experiencing the moment that was the culmination of his entire life. As he sat, staring into the steam that rose from that cup of coffee, he looked into every cup of coffee he had ever made. And for a brief time, he didn't feel so alone anymore, staring into his own reflection in the French press in front of him.

He poured the cream, he stirred the sugar with shaking hands, and the barista pretended he wasn't there, dragging his cleaning cloth over the countertop. Ricky looked over into the chair beside him and shook his head.

"What are you lookin' at?" he asked, and Bean tilted her head, watching him as he jabbed a finger out into the empty space. The barista lifted his eyes from the counter, but he didn't say anything.

Time passed slowly, and outside, the portal stirred to life, its activation roaring into the city streets while its lights flooded through the coffeehouse window. Ricky glanced up when the old man came to stand beside him, both of them gazing out toward the light. Ricky could still see the silhouettes of Porter and Sharkey in the distance.

"Holy hell," The barista muttered, shaking his head. "I didn't even know that thing worked. Ain't no one used that portal since I've been alive. No one ever contacts us, no one ever comes back." The old man shook his head and turned back toward the counter he'd left.

"Damn shame," he muttered to himself. "If ya ask me, the thing just killed 'em all."

Ricky stared into the street through the window, realizing slowly what the old man's words meant and what he still had left to do.

"Well, I ain't drinkin' it now," he muttered, shoving the cup of coffee toward the side and nodding to the empty chair.

"You drink it, I still got somethin' to do."

Then he stood, and the coffee sat untouched on the table where it had been set. The barista watched him as he rose and stepped out into the street, that little bell jingling as the door fell back against the frame.

Ricky took a breath of the air outside, looking down at Bean, whose gray muzzle had a smile on it despite everything she'd seen.

"Well, old girl, looks like we ain't done yet…now what're you gonna do? You can stay with him, or come with me." She barked in reply, pushing her head into his hand, and with that, he turned his back on the little coffee shop, on the city wall where he'd come through, on The Nothing, and Ricky and Bean walked into the portal together.

THE END

Made in the USA
Columbia, SC
16 September 2021